EARTHSTAR

Earthstar

Is it possible, we could have done something different,
something that could have changed our lives forever?
We are sending this recording into outer space in
hopes that whoever finds it will listen to it and avoid
making the same mistakes we made.

Sincerely,

The Explorers Club

TABLE OF CONTENTS

DEDICATION

This book is dedicated to my husband Reginald, my children and my family for supporting and encouraging me. Special thanks to Terry Thomas and Anthony Winston.

EARTHSTAR
Chapter 1—Changes

It was late August and the temperature had yet to reach eighty-five degrees. The summer nights had been quite cool. A strange air surrounded the town but no one seemed to notice. Enich Hills, Tennessee was a quiet little southern town. It had one church, post office, hospital and fire station. One of everything, that's all it really needed.

It was a long drive to Polaris Laboratories. Pam had put in six hours of overtime. The only thing she was thinking about was getting through the day, going home and spending a nice quiet evening with Adam.

 Pam grew tired of watching the endless rows of barbed wire fencing that lined both sides of the road. The agricultural center was on one side of the road and fields lined the other. Although Pam had driven this same road every night for ten years, somehow tonight it seemed different.

"Maybe," she thought. "All of this overtime is getting the best of me. I've got to ask Paul about getting some time off. It's not that I don't appreciate my job. Ten years ago the only thing people in this town had to look forward to was leaving."

"When Polaris Laboratories, a special division of the Institute of Space Studies and Advancement, decided to build their new facilities in Enich Hills; It opened up a whole new world for us, maybe too new. Polaris Labs bought over a thousand acres outside of town."

"There aren't many locals working for Polaris Labs. I guess my six years of college and working long hard hours at government labs finally paid off. Actually, I believe it was my Engineering degree that got me the job." Pam smiled as she drove her car down the newly paved streets of Polaris Labs. "I guess I'm lucky after all."

The bright headlights of an old BMW approached the gates of Polaris Labs. "Good morning, Mr. Stanton. May I see your I.D. please?" A tall muscular guard, who looked as if he had just come back from a Florida vacation, leaned in the car's window.

"When are you going to get rid of this old machine?"

"Old!" Adam replied. "This is a classic." Adam placed his I.D. back into his pocket and proceeded through the gate. This was the only entrance to Polaris Labs and it was under heavy surveillance.

Pamela Knight glanced between the huge stacks of papers on her desk. Adam leaned in the doorway. "What's with all the papers?" Pam smiled. To her, Adam was the perfect image of manhood. His dark hair, neatly trimmed mustache and rugged features were enough to make any woman stop and take notice. His strange eyes always seemed to twinkle.
"We are going to receive new security cards. Polaris Labs are being divided into color-coded sectors. The cards will tell the computers what sectors you are allowed to enter. Not to mention, your job title, health status, underwear size and everything else Polaris wants to know about you", she joked.

"I don't like the separatism or the thought of being controlled. Adam, why don't you escort me to the lounge?"

The elevator was crowded, so they climbed four flights of stairs. Adam opened the heavy yellow doors marked four. The chaotic sounds of construction bombarded them as they entered the hall. The bright fluorescent lights overhead gave the hall, the sterile look of a hospital. Construction workers with security clearance seemed to be everywhere. Red plastic nameplates were replacing the old black and white ones. The new security system was being installed quickly.

Pam and Adam knocked on a door with the old nameplate still attached.

"Come in! Come in!" A familiar voice barked hoarsely from the corner of the room. The voice belonged to Professor Donovan. He was nicely built for his age. He had snow-white hair and a handle bar mustache. It was hard to believe he was sixty-five.

Pam glanced at the nameplate on the desk. She looked at Adam and smiled softly. Her mind flashed back to that Sunday morning, four years ago when she and Adam walked home together for the first time. It was a brisk fall evening. A cool wind slightly chilled their bodies. The couple snuggled close to keep warm. Colorful autumn leaves danced a waltz in the breeze before drifting softly to the ground. Adam had talked continuously of his admiration for Professor Donovan.

A loud crash brought Pam's mind back to reality. She looked out of the office door and saw the remains of what had once been the east wall. Professor Donovan waved good-bye to Pam and Adam after a lengthy conversation. Adam briefly kissed Pam and then she headed towards the lounge. Life hadn't exactly been easy for Pam. She wasn't outgoing; in fact Adam was her first boyfriend. It seemed strange. Pam was not bad looking. She had a nice figure, a wonderful personality and a smile that would make the most deplorable person happy. Yet, somehow she remained friendless and dateless. "It'll all change someday," her mother would say. "Anything worth having is worth waiting for." "Is Adam worth waiting for?" Pam wondered. Their relationship had survived many problems. She'd met Adam at her sister's dinner party.

 Pam despised Adam immediately. She never understood how he knew exactly what to say to make her feel at ease. Since that time, Adam had married and divorced a woman he'd only known one month. He left behind his ex-wife, her two year old child and a heart broken Pamela Knight.
Pam was ecstatic when Adam's divorce was granted. Her joy was short lived. Two days later, her parents were killed in a car wreck. Their luxury car was crushed beneath a dump truck. The police report said they'd died instantly.

"Pam," a voice yelled.

"I'm sorry." She apologized. "How's your mother?" "She's fine." Nick smiled. "I won the science fair again." To Nick, this was no great accomplishment. He had lived in Polaris Town most of his life. He knew his way around the labs as well as any of the technicians or scientists.

Nick was one of the many young geniuses living in Polaris Town. When the labs were built, the I.S.S.A hired the best scientists, technicians and engineers. They also collected a number of young geniuses to attend Polaris Schools. They hoped to employ these youngsters one day.

 The activities around Polaris had been hectic for months. There were trucks, supplies and people scattered everywhere. The one person who seemed to stand out in the midst of the chaos was Nicholas Andropolus Cruz II. He was only five, but he immediately earned a special place in Pam's heart.

Nick was no longer a blushing five year old. He was now a handsome young man of fifteen. He was tall with beautiful wavy black hair, which he wore slightly longer than his school allowed. "I didn't mean to interrupt your thoughts; but I needed to talk to someone who would not think of me as a crazy kid. Nick's eyes seemed to plead for an unbiased ear.

Pam and Nick walked down the stairs to her office. She sat at her computer and began to type. "Go away Nicky. I've got a lot to do."

"But, Pam," he pleaded. "This is important."

"Aw right, Mr. Cruz. Start talking."

Nick removed several stacks of papers from a folding chair. "Have you noticed how strange the weather has been?" "

Did you come here to talk about the weather?" Pam interrupted.

"No!" Nick was getting frustrated. "I thought you would be willing to listen to me."
Pam realized how serious Nick was.

"I apologize, Nicky. I am just tired of all this extra work. I'll make you a deal. You help me file all these papers; clean the office and I'll treat you to lunch. There's a nice little beach outside of Enich Hills. It's a quiet spot and we can talk peacefully. Well, how about it?"

"Cool," Nick smiled.

Adam pushed the arrow pointing down, to summon the elevator. The elevator doors opened instantly. The morning rush was over and the elevators were easily accessible. A sign above the basement button read: NO UNAUTHORIZED ADMITTANCE! He pushed the button and wondered what new changes awaited him in the basement. Two minutes later, he had his answer. The elevator doors opened to reveal a large neon sign with two arrows. A yellow one, which read caution, pointed to the left. A green one read danger and pointed to the right. Beneath the sign was a small mahogany desk. A large black guard with a clean-shaven head sat quietly behind the desk. He looked up when the elevator doors opened.

"Morning Adam got a little gift for you." The guard smiled, extending his hand towards Adam. Adam took the rainbow colored security card, then placed it into a clear badge cover pinned to his lab coat. "The rainbow card means you can enter all sectors regardless of their color." The guard yawned. "I guess you're one of the lucky ones."

Adam walked down the corridor to the right. He was astounded by the large steel doors ahead of him. "They must have installed them overnight." A sign on the left side of the door flashed: INSERT SECURITY CARD! He slid his card into the semi-circle device. The jagged edged doors slid apart.

"This looks like something from a science fiction movie." Adam walked down the newly painted halls. The large steel doors slammed together behind him. Twelve doors and a right turn led him to another set of steel doors. ONLY RAINBOW CARDS BEYOND THIS POINT! The large sign above the door flashed hypnotically. He inserted his security card into the slot.

"Voice identification required." Surprisingly, he stammered his name.

"You may enter."

Pam and Nick walked across the parking lot to her midnight blue Jaguar. She unlocked the doors and slid behind the wheel. The soft sable seat covers made her feel luxuriant. They drove past Pam's house and then turned onto highway fifty-four. It felt good being away from the pressures and hassles of Polaris. Nick glanced out the window. "I hope Dr. Masters doesn't find out I'm skipping class. I really can't afford to get into any more trouble with Dad."

Dr. Nicholas Andropolus Cruz expected perfection from his son. Dr. Cruz graduated Summa Cum Laude from Harvard University. He completed his education at the age of fifteen. Two years later, he was second in command at the Aero Nautical Space Center. The walls of his office boasted of numerous awards including three Nobel prizes. Eleven years ago, he discovered a new solar system. There were several planets capable of sustaining human life. A man of his statue expected great things from his offspring. Nicholas II was similar to his father when it came to being a genius. That's where the similarities began and ended. Nick was a fun loving teenager, full of antics. Polaris High School had threatened to expel him several times.

"If you weren't so brilliant, I'd throw you out on your ass!" The principal yelled at him constantly. Nick knew the real reason he hadn't been expelled. He was the son of the founder of Polaris Town.

Pam parked her car on a narrow strip of manmade beach. They walked across a shaky wooden bridge to a small sand covered boardwalk. She was glad; she'd changed clothes before leaving Polaris. The wind played fondly with her hair. Nick noticed for the first time, how attractive Pam was. Her curved figure was neatly defined in her tight jeans. "And breasts!" It's amazing what a lab coat can hide."

He carried a small red cooler, which contained their lunch. An Army blanket was draped across his shoulders. It smelled like the motorcycle, it once covered. Pam pointed to an old dock extending into the water.

"That's where we'll eat." The dock creaked loudly with each step. "I assure you, it's safe." Pam laughed at the nervous expression on Nick's face. Nick stared blankly at the scenery. A half-eaten sandwich dropped from his hands. He blindly reached for the sandwich and began to talk.

"For years people complained about The Greenhouse Effect. The thought of Solar Radiation being absorbed by the Earth and the Earth not being capable of dissipating it worried a lot of people. Then about eight years ago, people stopped complaining. The threat of the Earth being burnt to a cinder just faded away. How is it that for year's major scientists and astronomers couldn't solve this problem? Then in the year two thousand twenty-five, all of our environmental problems are solved. Now, doesn't that strike you as kind of strange?"

"Not really," Pam swallowed.

"Think Pam! You're not being open-minded. Eleven years ago my Dad made a scientific break-through. Ten years ago, Polaris came to be; two years later, The Greenhouse Effect ended."

"Nick, are you trying to say Polaris Labs and your father had something to do with correcting The Greenhouse Effect? And if so, what's wrong with that?"

Nick yelled. "All of a sudden, Polaris decided to change access codes in the middle of a project. Dr. Weisman helped build Polaris and now he's only allowed in the blue sectors."

"I'd like to believe you, Nick," Pam said, stuffing trash into the cooler. "But, everything you've told me could simply be a coincidence, and even if it isn't; there's nothing malicious about it. You have no proof any wrong has or will be done."

"If I can prove foul play, will you believe me?"

"Sure Nick, now it's time to get back."

Adam was extremely agitated. "Why would Polaris make changes in the middle of a project? The Nebula II is scheduled for lift off in three weeks. There is no way we can be ready on time with construction workers constantly under foot. Cutting and hammering, it's just too many damn distractions. The Nebula I took off less than one week ago. What the hell is Nicholas Cruz trying to do? Set a record for the most space flights in a month."

The Nebulas were the most advanced methods of space travel. Their unique design and light weight enabled them to make several trips a month. They used a highly developed fuel called Proteus Transuranium. A few years earlier, Transuranium was regarded as a highly unstable element; which could not be used as an acceptable form of energy. The Conservation of Energy Law states that energy can be altered or changed but never destroyed. Scientists using a process based on this fact, called Proteus, were able to discover a way to alternate sources of energy. The result was a fuel that recycles itself.

The Nebulas were designed to carry large groups of scientists, technicians and their families on long space voyages. Adam wondered why the Nebula's crews were so small during the last trips. For the first time, family members were not allowed on the ships or to watch the launches. The rainbow line on Adam's phone glowed. The sound of the ringer startled him. He was not familiar with the new phone systems. The phone had different colors and tones for each sector.

"Stanton," Adam answered.

"Stanton, this is Donovan. We need you in the rainbow sector immediately."

"But I haven't finished the new design," Adam explained.

"I know." Professor Donovan replied. "You'll have to start working double time on this project. Time is running out. I'll see you in the lab."

The dial tone hummed in Adam's ear. "This is getting to be too much." He walked down the hall towards the rainbow sector.

Nick waved to his friends, as Pam pulled into the parking lot.

"Nick," she smiled. "If I were you, I'd concentrate more on my studies and less on "The Great Polaris Mystery."

"Yeah right." Nick hurried out the car and joined his friends.

Tia, Max and Angie Faye were members of The Explorers Club. The Explorers were the best students in scientific studies and experimentation. The other members were Lenny Peterson, Reginald Norwin, Charles Bradford, sometimes called The Brain and the last member was Nicholas Cruz II.

"What did Dr. Masters say about my absence from class?" "He never realized you were missing." Tia laughed. "We got Toby Chandler to answer for you. Toby will do anything to become an Explorer."

The four friends decided to go to the malt shop instead of English Literature.
Nicholas!" A voice yelled sternly.

"Oh shit! It's your father. We'll see you at the malt shop. That is, if you can make it." Max waved, as he and the others headed towards Polaris mall.

"Uh, hi Dad." Nick nervously approached his father. "What's up Dad?"

"Why aren't you in class?" Nick knew his father's punishments were unbearable.

"I was between classes," he lied. "So, I decided to catch up with Max and get his notes on the science project, we're doing together."

His father looked skeptical. "Tell your mother, I'm not coming home this evening. I've got a lot of work to catch up on. After you finish your classes for the day, bring me a change of clothes. Tell your mother, I'll be home tomorrow in time for dinner."

The malt shop was jamming with loud music. It appeared as if half of Polaris High's students were there. Nick opened the door of the malt shop. The loud noise and the smell of fast foods, hit him in the face. "Heaven," he thought. He glanced around the room. The flashing strobe lights made the black and white mosaic floor come to life. He spotted his friends at a table in the rear.

"What's shakin'?" Reggie asked. Nick sat in the chair next to Reggie.

"Thanks for ordering for me. Where's The Brain?" Lenny joined the group before Reggie could answer.

"Now you know The Brain isn't going to skip class for anyone." He swallowed. "I got to talk to you guys about something important," Nick stated. "It must be important," Tia laughed. "Look who just stepped in the door?"

A young blonde kid with rounded glasses stood in the doorway.

"He looks lost. Reggie, guide our lost sheep to the table." Max laughed. Reggie walked over to the door and touched Charles on the shoulder.

"What are you going to order Brain? And by the way, what wind blew you out of class?"

"Mr. Wells broke his foot and class was cancelled." The Brain said.

"That figures," Tia smirked.

"I can't order anything this close to dinner time." The Brain sighed.

"Oh, come on. This is the beginning of the Labor Day weekend and everyone is chowing down." Angie Faye cringed. "Doesn't your Mom ever let up?"

"She just wants what's best for me." The Brain smirked.

"Hey chill everyone!" Nick yelled. "I'm calling this meeting of the Explorers Club to order. I feel that Polaris is up to no good. But, I need proof."

Pam glanced at her office door as it creaked open. Adam sat on her desk and rubbed a rose across her face.

"Is that all I get?" Pam asked. Adam leaned over and lightly touched his lips to hers. A few seconds later, they were lost in a passionate kiss. "I can't wait for tonight," she whispered.

"That's what I came to talk to you about, Pam. Dr. Cruz has made it mandatory for all technicians and scientists to spend the night working at the labs. I'm sorry."

She stared out her office window. "I was looking forward to spending time with you. I love you Adam."

"Aw, you're just saying that because you're upset."

"No! I really love you. I just wanted to tell you at the right moment." Pam dropped her head.

"It is the right moment. I love you too. I'll make it up to you. I promise." Adam smiled.

Nick stepped out the elevator and flashed his school badge to the guard. "My Dad is expecting me."

"All right Mr. Cruz. Here's a temporary rainbow pass."

Nick walked down the green sector's corridor. He laughed at the warning sign above the rainbow sector's doors. His card eased into the slot and the doors slid open. A five second alarm sounded when his feet touched the rainbow colored tile. An armed guard swerved quickly. His automatic rifle pointed towards Nick's head.

"W-What the hell is going on here?" Nick slowly held up his rainbow pass. The guard called Dr. Cruz to confirm Nick's visit.

"Carry on," he said sternly.

Nick was still shaking when he arrived at his father's office.

"I brought your clothes, Dad."

"Sit down a minute," his father said, handing him a cola. "I need you to take these papers to Dr. Quartz's office. Her office is the third door on the left."
Nick knocked on Dr. Quartz's door. She opened it immediately. After exchanging greetings, Nick handed her the papers.

"There's an exit door at the end of the hall. Where does it go?"

"It leads to a field near the parking lot behind your school." Dr. Quartz answered.

"Does it have security locks too?" Nick asked.

"Yes, but why are you so curious?" She asked.

"I guess, I'm just proud of the new security system," he lied. "Is there a guard on that door, since it's so far down the hall?"

"No one's been assigned to it yet. Well I'd love to keep talking, but I've got a lot of work to do." Dr. Quartz pushed Nick out of her office.

Nick ran back to his father's office. "D-Dad," he stammered. "Do I have to leave the same way, I came in? I have a lot of homework to do and I have to finish my science project over the weekend. If I have to deal with that armed guard again; I'm not sure I'll be able to study at all."

He knew how to worry his father. Just the thought of Nick, not functioning education wise, could ruin his father's day.

"Well Nick," His father said, forgetting about the rainbow pass. "I'll let you out the back door." Nick's father had played right into Nick's hands. Now with the rainbow card, he'd have access to the labs and the computer file rooms. All he had to do now was figure a way to get past the guards.

Pam glanced at the clock. The bright green digital numbers seemed to glow unnaturally. "Nine fifty five. I shouldn't be lying in bed alone. Dr. Cruz has never pulled a stunt like this, not even when the Nebulas were behind schedule. All right Pam, get a hold of yourself. You're letting a little horniness make you crazy. The next thing you know, you'll be thinking like Nick."

Nick was slowly falling asleep. He was startled by a loud howling sound beneath his window. Max was hiding in the bushes below Nick's window. Nick climbed out the window and onto the tree limb. He scurried down the tree as fast as he could.

"Let's go Max." They left their quiet little neighborhood behind and headed toward Polaris Center.

"Yo Nick, do you ever get the feeling of being locked up?" Max asked.

"What do you mean Max?"

"I mean everything we do revolve around Polaris Labs. Our homes, schools, everything is inside this big fence; the locals call Polaris Town. I haven't left Polaris Town since we moved here, eight years ago. Don't get me wrong. I enjoy my life and all of our friends. It's like living in a small town and knowing there's something bigger and better out there."

"I guess I never thought of it that way. You're right, even our schools enforce the idea of growing up and becoming a part of the Polaris work force." Nick glanced at the sky and thought about the world outside of Polaris Town.

"Nick, have you ever thought about what happens to the students who don't fit into Polaris' society?" Max asked.

"I don't know," Nick said, while climbing the fence at Polaris Center.

The boys jumped off the top of the fence, landing in the soft Bermuda grass on the other side. A beam of light flashed in several windows. The guards were making their rounds. Polaris encouraged their young minds. However, they didn't want them learning too much, in case they decided to leave Polaris.

"Get down, he'll see you!" Max whispered. "When the light in the third window goes out, we'll head towards the back window."

The Brain was waiting for them under the window.

"I set the computer, so the alarm would turn off at ten fifteen. It will only be off for sixty seconds. That should give us enough time to get in. It will turn off again at ten forty five. We will have thirty minutes to search the computers."

"That may not be enough time," Max complained.

"I know, but that's all the time we've got," The Brain mumbled. "The technicians come in at eleven. I'll need time to alter the alarm's program. We don't want anyone to know, it was off for a few minutes."

The lights in the building flickered for one brief moment. It was time. The three boys moved quickly towards the back door. Max removed the key card from his pocket; the key card, he'd stolen just four hours earlier from his father's desk. The click of the lock seemed to echo throughout the night. The door seemed to creak unusually loud. Max closed the door carefully and locked it. The guard never heard a sound. He was eating a ham sandwich and watching the pre-season football games.

He yelled, as if on cue. "That's it, that's it. Run with it. Run with it. All right, that's the way to play!"

The boys ran quietly down the opposite hall. The computer room was four doors down. Max unlocked the door. They entered and silently closed the door.

"How did you know the guard would not be watching the monitors?" Max asked.

"He's a friend of my Dad's and he's addicted to sports."

The Brain removed the computer's cover. "Let's get started. Leave the lights off; the computer will provide enough light."

Max placed his jacket over the door's window. Nick handed him two thumbtacks.

"Good thinking," Max smiled.

The computer whirred to life. The Brain and the computer appeared to be as one. He typed away at the keyboard, bypassing code after code. Finally, he reached the R-Zone.

"Got it," he grinned.

A rainbow flashed on the screen. Beneath it, the words: ABSOLUTELLY NO UNAUTHORIZED ENTRY appeared. The words flashed brightly and then the screen went blank.

"Oh shit!" Max whispered.

Suddenly, the screen blinked back on. ENTER SECURTIY CODE flashed on the screen. "You have five minutes before the alarm sounds," a computerized voice said.

"What if we can't break the code and decide to cancel the program?" Max asked.

Nick slashed his finger across his throat.

"I know the code has something to do with the rainbow," Nick said.

Bleep, bleep, bleep, access denied the computer flashed.

Four minutes and ten seconds appeared at the bottom of the screen.

"Think, you guys!" The Brain drummed nervously on the computer.

"The pot of gold at the end of the rainbow." Max grinned.

"It's worth a try." The Brain typed as fast as he could.

"Bleep, bleep, bleep, access denied." They all chimed. Three minutes and counting appeared on the bottom of the screen.

The sound of footsteps approaching the door startled the boys.

"Damn! It's the guard. What are we gonna do? If we get caught, we're up shit creek."

Max reached up and made sure the door was locked. Time was ticking away on the computer. The Brain couldn't risk the computer bleeping. The doorknob turned slowly, then clicked. Realizing the door was locked, the guard moved on.

"Whew!" They exclaimed.

"We've got less than a minute," Nick shrieked. "There are just too many things it could be, to many secrets."

"That's it!" The Brain exclaimed quietly.

The seconds were ticking away. He quickly typed: THE SECRET UNDER THE RAINBOW. The screen blinked. The colors of the rainbow slowly flashed on the screen. A blank rainbow stretched across the screen. One by one the spectral colors assumed their places on the rainbow. Under the right end of the rainbow, the word secret appeared.

The screen went blank, and then a list appeared:
Number One-Nebulas I and II, Number Two-Synacom
14/Earthstar, Number Three-Orion/Colossus/Argon,
Number four-Artec.

"Where do we start?" The Brain asked.

"We already know about the Nebulas, so let's start
with number two." Max suggested.

"Two it is," The Brain smiled.

The screen blinked twice. The words Synacom 14 and
Earthstar appeared on the screen. The screen blinked
once more.

"It's a diagram of some kind of space station," Max
grinned proudly. The diagram was circular with star-
like tentacles. The diagram rotated showing Earthstar
from several angles. The height, width and weight
flashed across the bottom of the screen.

"That's impossible! How could something that massive weigh so little? Check this out." Max pointed to the upper right hand corner of the screen. "This space station was built from a type of metal called Synacom 14. Am I dumb? Or is there no such thing as Synacom 14?" The screen flashed more and more information. The lights in the building dimmed for one second.

"Man, we completely forgot about the time," screeched The Brain. "I've got to clear up everything. We have less than five minutes to get out of here!"

I hate this," Max sighed. "There's so much we haven't learned."

Within five minutes, the boys had departed the building, leaving no traces of their visit.

Chapter 2

Pam snuggled under the covers. She loved sleeping late on Saturdays. It was sixty-three degrees. The weatherman promised it would remain in the lower seventies. She glanced at the clock. The green digital numbers, not so bright in the morning sunlight, clearly read eleven forty-five AM. Forcing herself out of bed was not easy. Pam pushed the curtains apart and opened the blinds. The sun's rays illuminated the room like a high intensity light bulb. Shielding her eyes from the bright light, she reached for the phone.

"This is a recorded message. Adam is not…" She hung up the phone. Adam was still at Polaris. Pam decided to shower and go to Polaris Mall. She hoped to run into Adam, somewhere in Polaris Town.

Nick had nearly finished cutting the yard, when the mower cut off. "Well," Nick said to his mother. "I guess the mower is too hot. I'll have to finish the yard later."

Mrs. Cruz walked over to the mower and removed the gas cap. "To hot huh?"

"Aw Mom, I got to meet the guys at the mall for lunch. It's nearly twelve."

"All right Nick, I'll finish the yard…*this time*," she emphasized. Nick ran towards the house. He glanced back at his mother. She didn't seem like the motherly type. She was a good mother, but she was also a friend. Nick closed the door and ran upstairs. The feeling of being watched crept over Mrs. Cruz. She looked behind her. Lenny Peterson was leaning against the mailbox, staring at her buttocks.

"Like the shorts," he grinned. "Nick still here?"

"He's in the shower. Go in and wait for him, please!" She laughed.

Lenny entered the Stained Glass doors. A short hall led to the foyer. Aquariums were built into each wall of the foyer. In the center of the floor was a fifty-gallon tank on a Cherry Wood stand. There were two narrow doors on the left and right walls. Lenny assumed Dr. Cruz cleaned the tanks and fed the fish from there. The aquariums were decorated with Old Clipper Ships, seaweed and castles built of coral. It was like stepping into an underwater world.

Lenny walked towards the spiral staircase near the foyer entrance. He climbed the stairs two at a time. The third door on the right had a sign that read: UNNATURAL INHABITANT— ENTER AT YOUR OWN RISK! Lenny opened the door. Three hundred and twenty watts of hard rock nearly blasted him back into the hall. In the background of the music, he could barely hear the faint sound of the shower. Lenny turned the music down and pushed the bathroom door open.

"Yo Nick," he yelled. "Hurry up man. I've got some awesome news."

"All right. Give me a few minutes." Nick yelled. Lenny fumbled through a stack of compact discs on the bed. A few seconds later, Nick stepped into the room wearing black underwear. He removed an old pair of blue jeans from the closet.

"Throw me that Tee shirt from the top drawer."

Nick dressed quickly, and then slipped on a new pair of sneakers. Lenny fidgeted on the bed.

"Did you hear about the Harrison's?"

"What about them?" Nick asked.

"They're gone." Lenny stated.

"Gone where?" Nick combed through his hair unconcerned.

"Gone, I mean, like they don't live at five twenty one Draco, anymore."

"So," Nick remarked.

"Look stupid." Lenny was getting angry. "There's already another family living there. No one seems to know anything. It's like they just disappeared off the face of the Earth, then another family took their place. No one just up and leaves Polaris Town overnight. I asked Jimmy, the guard at the gate. He said no one has moved out of Polaris Town since it's been here. Now you tell me. What happened to the Harrison's?"

 "Who cares?" Nick said, rushing out the door. "Let's go."

    Polaris Mall was not very large, but it was adequate. The mall was enclosed, so the temperature was always consistent. Pam walked over to one of the open eating areas. The Canis Canteen, The Altair Diner and Sirius Burgers were a few of the open restaurants. Pam decided to order the Bright Star Platter and a cherry cola. When her order was ready, she sat at her usual table.

"May I join you?" A voice asked.

"Why Mr. Stanton, I'd be honored." Pam teased. Adam placed his tray on the table. He had a rough night and Pam knew it.

"What time will you get off?" She questioned nibbling on an onion ring.

"I'm off now. I decided to stop for lunch, before calling you," he said. "We can spend the rest of the weekend together, starting now."

The members of The Explorers Club were seated at two round tables near the end of the open eating area. "Did you guys hear about Ricky Schaeffer's family?" Reggie swallowed, and then wiped his mouth on the napkin Tia handed him. "This pizza is great. Well, anyway it seems as though he and his family just vanished last night."

Nick's slice of pizza fell to the floor. "The Harrison's are gone too. What's going on?" Tia gasped.

"Brain, what did you find out from the computer, last night."

"Apparently not enough," The Brain commented.

"Someone's already living in Ricky's house. Isn't that queer? We've got to get to the bottom of this," Reggie stated.

"We may be the next ones to disappear. Say Brain, does Polaris Techs check the computers on Saturday nights?" Max questioned.

"Yeah," The Brain smiled. "I mean no, most of Polaris' workers will be off for the rest of the holiday weekend. We can tell our parents we're camping out. We can sneak into Polaris Center and find out what's going on.

"Nick, do you still have that rainbow pass?" Angie Faye asked.

Nick nodded his head. He knew the disappearances were only the beginning. He felt sure Polaris Town and Enich Hills were in for a rough ride. Pam and Adam were preparing to leave the mall.

"I'll be back in a minute," Nick told his friends. He ran towards Pam and Adam. "Hi, Dr. Stanton. Hi, Pam. Pam, I really need to talk to you."

"Not now Nicky," Pam mumbled.

"Then when?" Nick waited for an answer.

"Not this weekend. I've got plans, besides nothing can be that important, right?" Nick knew Pam was serious.

"Right, hundreds of lives don't count for shit." He grumbled and then walked off.

 "What's with Nick?" Adam puzzled.

"Maybe, he's a little jealous," Pam teased.

"Why should he be jealous?" Adam asked.

"Well," she teased. "I had to spend my spare time with someone, since you weren't around." They both laughed happily, as they exited the mall. Still, Pam couldn't help feeling uneasy because of what Nick said.

    A cold wind slapped Pam's face. She glanced at the quartz sign in the center of the parking lot. The sign flashed the time and temperature. Two fifteen, fifty-eight degrees. "Wow!" Pam thought. The temperature had actually dropped. Adam put his arms around Pam and hurried towards her car. Pam glanced in the rear view mirror. She could see Adam still watching, as she drove away. Pam knew he was going to follow her home, but the uneasiness continued to grow. "Damn that Nick! He is going to ruin my weekend, one way or another."

The wind roared in unison with the thunderclaps. The sound of rain pelting against the window blended in perfectly with the cracking of the logs in the fireplace. She couldn't have asked for a better evening. Adam was sleeping peacefully, with his head in her lap. Her fingers danced playfully through his hair. She tried to keep her mind on Adam, but thoughts of Nick kept running through her mind.

The storm had altered the Explorer's plans. They stayed home, leaving The Brain and Nick with the dirty work. They were positive; the guard would be more relaxed tonight. Who would think someone would be out on a night like this? The lightning flashed, as the computer whirred to life. Nick and The Brain learned more and more about the space station called Earthstar.

"Talk about a world project," Nick whispered. "It appears all of the top men in the world are involved. The leaders of China, Japan and several other nations are participating. The new Pope is also involved. Pope Solomon Micah, one of the most respected men of all times. There's a lot of power behind this. This is no ordinary space project."

The Brain gasped, "Look at the names of the latest inhabitants of Earthstar. The Harrison's, the Schaeffer's and a family named Symthe; so much for the missing families." The screen blinked. Enter rainbow code now to continue.

"What are we gonna do? We don't have the code." The Brain looked at Nick for an answer. Nick pushed the cancel button.

"We have to get that code." "I just hope we can pull that off," The Brain grumbled.

A loud clap of thunder startled them. "We'd better head home before this gets any worse," Nick said. The boys climbed the fence and headed home. "Call me tomorrow after church!" Nick yelled. Nick climbed the tree and crawled along the branch that led to his window. He turned on the shower and removed his wet clothing. Snuggling under the covers, he thought; "I'll never fall asleep. I'm too excited." Nick was sound asleep before his head hit the pillow.

Adam awoke to the sound of a loud thunderclap. Pam smiled, "how about a drink, sleepy head?" Adam nodded. She returned to the den carrying two glasses of wine. The last sparks flickered in the fireplace behind them as they closed the bedroom door.
Church service seemed to last forever. Glancing at his watch every few minutes only frustrated him. Nick was relieved when the services finally ended.

"Nick, you're awfully quiet," his mother commented.

"I've got a lot on my mind," he said.

"School work, I hope," his father stated.

"Nicholas Cruz," his wife said sternly. "The boy is on vacation. Give him a break."

The car pulled into the driveway. Nick's father hesitated before driving into the garage. "Nick," he stated. "I'm having very important guests tonight. I expect you to be on time for dinner and dressed appropriately."

"Dinner will be served at seven thirty," Mrs. Cruz smiled. "That gives you four hours to have fun."

Nick hurried to his room. He knew by now, the other members of The Explorers Club would know what happened last night. Nick phoned Reggie. Reggie answered on the first ring.

"Nick, your Dad's rainbow card has his fingerprints and code on it. If you sneak it out the house along with the temporary pass, Brain can duplicate your father's information onto the temporary card."

"My Dad's having dinner guests. So, even if I find the card, I won't have time to bring it to you." Nick complained.

"You find the card. I'll take of the rest. Give me a call when you are ready." Reggie hung up the phone.

Nick removed a wooden file box from his desk. The temporary pass was filed under K for key. He put the box back into the drawer. He would retrieve it later if he was lucky enough to get his father's card. He walked quietly down the stairs to his father's office. The door was open. His father was seated at a large antique roll top desk. The desk had an old-fashioned hurricane lamp and several files on it. The wall was covered with awards, degrees and certificates. A chair behind a smaller desk had a white jacket draped over it. The sun was reflecting off something on the left pocket. Nick knew that was what he was looking for, the rainbow card.

"D-Dad, after dinner will you and your guests be in here?"

"No, we'll be in the library. We've got business to discuss. I want you to find something to do to occupy your time for a couple of hours. I don't want you under foot."

 Dr. Cruz walked across the room. He removed his jacket from the desk.
 "Nick," he yawned. "Drop this jacket in the hamper." Nick reached for the jacket. "Hold it a minute," his father said. Dr. Cruz removed the rainbow card from his jacket. "Oh yeah, where's the temporary pass?" Nick's heart sank. His chance of getting more information had just ended.

"I'll find it and bring it to you in the morning, Dad."

"I need it tonight," Dr. Cruz exclaimed.

 Nick entered the nearest bathroom and tossed the jacket down the laundry chute. "Damn, now I've got to explain to the Explorers, how I screwed things up." Nick was lying across the bed in the dark, when the first guests began to arrive. He glanced at the clock on his DVD. Seven o'clock glowed in small digital letters. The beam from a car's headlights made eight square lights dance across the wall. He couldn't believe how much time had passed.

He had called Reggie, three hours ago. Then he crawled on his bed to think of an alternative plan. "I must have fallen asleep," he thought.

Dr. Cruz and his guests retired to the library after dinner. Nick listened outside the doors until his mother spotted him.

"Nick!" She scolded. "I taught you better." Nick apologized.

He knew his mother would never mention this incident to his father. She hated how severely angry he could be when it came to disciplining Nick, She had tried very hard to make him realize, Nick was a child prodigy but he was still a child. She'd met Dr. Cruz while working at the I.S.S.A. They were married six months after they met. Dr. Cruz didn't believe in putting off what needed to be done. She knew then, just as she knew now, he'd never change.

Nick had listened outside the library long enough to find out something was happening tomorrow night. "Aw yes, Labor Day." the perfect cover, almost everyone will be off work. What better time to do something sinister. It could go completely unnoticed.

Chapter 3

Pam awoke suddenly. She looked around the dark room. Sweat was dripping from her unclad body. Slowly, she began to realize where she was. She and Adam had gone out to dinner and then to the Lovable Pets Pet Shop. She had fallen in love with a little puppy. The little Alaskan malamute did his best performance. The sad eyes routine and all. Adam had teased her about the pup. Halfway home, the pup had an accident on Pam's skirt. Because of his accident, they named him Poseidon. Pam glanced at the clock, nine thirty three PM. She could hear soft murmurs coming from the den. "How sweet," she thought. Adam was doing his best not to awaken her.

"This is a dream that should last forever."

"Dream!" The sudden memory of her nightmare flooded through her mind so quickly, she could hardly catch her breath.

 It was very dark and cold. Pam felt so alone. Yet, she knew someone was watching her. She turned slowly and gasped. There was no one behind her; in fact there was nothing there. Polaris Town and all the surrounding areas had vanished. The silence was deafening. She felt cold, lonely and destined for insanity. Pam was beginning to panic. In the darkness, one lone streetlight glowed fiercely against the dark. It was as if it alone tried to fight against the eternal dark and emptiness. For one brief moment, Pam thought she saw a small man in the distance. The image quickly faded into the darkness.

A strange mechanical popping sound rang through her head. Turning in the direction of the sound, she saw nothing. She glanced over the horizon and there it was. A huge ball of fire hurled itself towards the Earth, like a fiery finger of death. She grabbed her chest as a cold arrow of fear penetrated her heart. The bright orange flames reflected off her hair and face. She stood trembling with fear. The fiery ball emitted a high-pitched sound as it entered the Earth's atmosphere. Pam heard a scream coming from the direction of the streetlight. She saw a man running towards her. The closer he got, the smaller he became.

"That's not a man, it's a boy!" "Nick," she screamed.

"It's too late! I tried to warn you!" He screamed pointing to the ball of fire.

The back of Pam's hair and neck started to singe. She turned around slowly. The fiery ball was the size of the Earth. It was so close, she felt she could reach up and touch it. The heat was so intense; she began to gasp for air. Her face burst into flames. The pain was unbearable. Flames engulfed her body. Through the flames and stench of her own flesh, she watched as Nick's body glowed orange and exploded. Just before the orange ball hit the Earth, she screamed. She never realized that as she screamed in the dream she screamed in reality.

Adam raced into the bedroom. "I was in the yard, when I heard you scream." He turned the dimmer switch. The room immediately flooded with light.

"Did I scream?" She asked. Adam sat on the bed and put his arms around her.

"You're trembling," he quieted. "Pam it was just a dream."

"Just a dream," she cried.

Nick called and emergency meeting of The Explorers Club. Sneaking out of the house in the middle of the night had become second nature to the Explorers.

"It's 11:30 pm. This meeting of The Explorers Club is now called to order." Angie Faye yawned and began to read the minutes of the last meeting. "The last meeting was held Friday at the mall.
Nick had a hunch. Club members decided to investigate. Thus far, we've proved Polaris is full of mysteries. Now the floor is open for discussion."

"Quiet everyone!" Nick yelled. "I think we should be prepared."

"Prepared for what?" Tia asked.

"What if," Nick gestured. "What if your family is the next to disappear? The Explorers were silent. "We know all of the families are being moved inconspicuously. I figure the families are being moved between two and four in the morning. If one of our families are moved, we could keep track of them."

"What good would that do?" Tia asked.

"We could keep track of where you're being moved."
"Right," Tia groaned. "So, we find out where they are going. What can we do to stop what's happening? We're just kids."

"Since, we don't know what's going on, we'll have to make decisions as we go. The transmitters Brain made for his computer should still work. I put them in one of those." Nick said, pointing to a stack of crates.

"Got 'em," Lenny smiled. The transmitters were shaped like the Greek letter Delta. It had a capital letter E in the center. The Brain had designed the transmitters as club pins. Until now, they had only been used to gather classified information about Polaris' rockets. The Explorers Club used this information to design, what they were calling the ultimate vehicle for space travel.

Nick walked over to a blackboard; he'd mischievously stolen from Polaris Center. He wrote: AT ALL TIMES! "Wear these as if your life depended on it! It just might. Brain, activate the system and leave it on. Everyone keep your cell phones on. Keep watching and listening. This meeting is adjourned."

A festive ambience filled the air. The parking lot of Polaris Mall had been transformed into a mini carnival. Games, rides, carnival foods and the sweet smell of cotton candy helped to build the excitement in Polaris Town. The entertainment committee was busy setting up fireworks displays. The fireworks and carnival lights would illuminate Polaris Town like a star in the night. There was something for everyone, from the youngest to the oldest.

Dr. Cruz had been working at the labs since six that morning. He and his special crew had arranged for Planetoid, the guest rock band to arrive in limos identical to the ones their guests would arrive in.

Pam handed Adam her I.D. as they approached the gates of Polaris Town. After checking their security cards they were allowed to enter Polaris Town. Pam glanced in the rear view mirror. A limousine was pulling up behind them. It seemed to stretch from the gates of Polaris Town to the end of the driveway.

"That's odd," she thought to herself.

"Not really," Adam replied, as if reading her mind. "There are two limos instead of one."

Pam parked in her usual parking space at Polaris Labs. They decided it would be better to walk to Polaris Mall. They didn't want to fight the crowds for parking spaces.

"Two limos, for a band that small? That's kind of weird." She glanced over her shoulders. The two limos went different ways.

"It's probably just a diversion to keep the kids from going wild." Adam laughed. "We'd better hurry. It's almost noon."

They'd volunteered to work at one of the concession stands from twelve until four. The crowds were already gathered around the pronto pup stand.

"I'm glad we're not working that one!" Pam gasped. "All of the concession stands will be just as crowded as that one." Adam smiled. "What have I gotten us into?"

Pam was horrified. She stared at the unbelievable crowds. She didn't realize there were so many people in Polaris Town. Adam unlocked the door to the cotton candy/candy apple stand. He read the instructions for the cotton candy machine. Someone had already made several huge bags of cotton candy. A carton of paper cones was underneath his chair. One flick of the switch and the cotton candy machine whirred into action. Adam poured the sugar into the machine. Pam placed the previously prepared candy apples in a display case. Thirty minutes later, they were open for business. Nick was their first customer. He volunteered to help until one thirty.

The crowds swarmed around the cotton candy/candy apple stand. An oscillating fan kept the small concession stand cool. Though, the temperature was only seventy-two degrees, the heat generated from the crowds made it feel hotter. Even though the crowds became a little hectic at times, the three vendors enjoyed their job tremendously. Nick glanced at his watch. It was two thirty.

"Man," he thought. "The time really flew. I've got to meet the Explorers. We're going to wait for Planetoid to arrive. They are supposed to be here at three." "They arrived before noon." Pam handed a little red haired boy a candy apple. "They arrived in two stretch limos." Pam said.

"Two!" Nick puzzled. "That's odd. Well, gotta run." Nick hurried towards the hill near Polaris' gates. The Explorers had been waiting since two o'clock.

"Why Nicholas Cruz," Angie Faye teased. "It's nice of you to honor us with your presence."

"Get real," Reggie frowned. "The last thing you need to do is add a southern accent to that country voice of yours." Everyone snickered.

"We missed Planetoid." Nick groaned. "They arrived around noon." The Explorers were disappointed. They decided to go back to the carnival for lunch. Afterwards, they would go to Reggie's house and play video games until dark. Reggie's family had the biggest game room in Polaris Town. Everything a teen could want. Pool tables, air hockey, virtual reality and more…

Adam and Pam left the cotton candy/candy apple stand at four thirty. Their replacements were a little late. Adam suggested they walk back to Polaris Labs to shower. They were so sticky, everything the wind blew past them, stuck to them. Pam was frivolously struggling to pull leaves from her sticky hair. "Thank God for automated doors. I would hate to walk around with a door knob stuck in my hands."

 The sound of their footsteps echoed throughout the empty halls of Polaris Labs. The deserted hallways felt eerie.

"It's uncanny!" Pam said. Adam unlocked his office door. "What's uncanny?" He flipped a switch to lighten his dark office.

"The fact that Polaris let everyone off for Labor Day; including guards."

Adam turned on the water in the double Jacuzzi. They undressed and immersed their bodies in the warm water. Pam immediately reached for the shampoo. Thirty minutes later, she slipped into a pair of jeans and a tee shirt. "Keeping extra clothing around here comes in handy," she laughed. "I think I'll take a walk down the hall while you get dressed." She knew Adam would take forever to get dressed.

Half way down the hall, she began to hear voices.

"That's impossible. No one's supposed to be in the building." The closer she got to the end of the hall, the louder the voices became. "Someone is in this building. What am I going to do? I don't have clearance." She leaned closer to the door. Although the thick metal door muffled the voices, one voice stood out above the rest.

"It will take off on time. I assure you." Dr. Cruz had a distinguishable voice. It was a masculine take charge type of voice. To her, his voice was like a thunderous command from God.

"Are you sure, it will blend in?" A voice asked. This voice was also familiar; although it wasn't the voice of someone she knew, personally.

"It is easier to show you than to explain it to you." Another familiar voice said.

Chairs began to move around in the room.

"Oh shit! They're coming out. There isn't enough time to run back to Adam's office. She hid behind a stone pillar, praying that Adam would not come looking for her.

The group led by Professor Donovan, walked past the pillar. They never noticed Pam's shadow extending across the floor towards them. She wanted to look and see who the other people were, but she was too afraid. The exit door closed with a bang. Pam ran down the hall to Adam's office. She tried to tell him what she'd heard, but he brushed it off. He told her she was letting Nick get to her. As they left the building, Pam wondered if Nick could really be right.

A warm breeze danced through her hair. The sun felt good and she decided to take advantage of it. "Let's have dinner at The Outdoor Café." The Outdoor Café was a fifteen minute drive from Polaris Town. They had the best seafood in the south. The midnight blue jaguar seemed to glide down the highway on a cushion of air. Pam loved driving with the top down. She pulled into the parking lot at six twenty. The Outdoor café was crowded.

A manmade lake surrounded the restaurant. The hostess led them across a rope bridge to a table near the waterfall. A nice breeze was blowing across the lake. It would be dark soon and The Outdoor Café would come to life. The lake would reflect the light from the glowing lanterns like a dark mirror. Bands would play and the dance floor would be full of people. It was a wonderful place to be at night. A short stocky waitress lit the candles on their table, while another served dinner. Adam leaned over and kissed Pam. "This is your night," he smiled

Pam hoped Adam would want to stay at the restaurant a little longer. She did not want to return to the carnival. After dinner, they rented a paddleboat. Later, they danced. At eight o'clock, Adam suggested returning to the carnival. Pam was disappointed until she remembered the voices. "Maybe," she thought. "I'll find out something."

The Explorers returned to the carnival at seven thirty. The carnival was lit up brilliantly. Reggie suggested riding the Loop-de-loop, first. The line was long but the ride was worth it. They stood in line nearly twenty minutes to ride the roller coaster. It was the most popular ride at the carnival. Nick enjoyed the rides, but he was looking around constantly. The Explorers knew he was looking for Steffie Donovan.

Stephanie Michelle Donovan moved to Polaris, four months ago. Her father was killed in a lab explosion at the I.S.S.A. Her grandfather insisted she and her mother come to live with him. Nick had fallen hopelessly in love with her.
 Angie Faye and Tia led the Explorers towards the Giant Waterslide. The line was short and the

splashing water was refreshing. The Fierce Farris wheel was next. They could see the entire carnival from the top. The Farris wheel stopped with Reggie and Tia at the top. Nick was seated below them. He looked down at the carnival, but he didn't see Steffie. When the ride was over, they entered the house of mirrors. It was a two-story structure that was just as hard to get into, as it was to get out of. After three minutes, they advanced to the second floor. Nick stared out the window. Someone patted him on the back.

"Cheer up, this is a carnival. It's supposed to be fun."

Nick turned around and there she was, Steffie Donovan. She had beautiful curly brown hair. Her dimples and green eyes lit up her face when she smiled. Nick was speechless.

"Aw right!" Reggie walked past them and smiled. "Let's get out of here and go to the Labyrinth. Then we can ride in the tunnel of love." He stared at his reflection in one of the mirrors. His tall bronze muscular body proved weights and exercise could really make a difference. He was once a skinny black kid, who looked more like a nerd than the Brain. Reggie prided himself on his athletic ability. Getting noticed was the last thing he had to worry about. Every girl at Polaris High knew him, and most had daydreamed about him. There weren't many black families living in Polaris Town. Polaris Town consisted of less than one fourth minorities. Being black didn't seem to matter in Polaris Town. Everyone was a member of one race, the Polaris Town race.

Adam and Pam arrived at the carnival at nine o'clock.
They entered the freak show, a few minutes ahead of
the Explorers. Watching the teens clown around
eased Pam's mind; how could she have taken anything
seriously from someone who acts like them? A loud
bang interrupted her thoughts. Everyone wondered if
the fireworks had begun early. A giant three-headed
snake, soon made the audience forget the loud noise.
The ten-foot python had two heads at one end and one
on the other. People were picked from the audience to
check it for authenticity. The show lasted twenty
minutes.

 The majority of the audience crowded into the next
tent. The show was called The Magnificent World of
Sea Creatures. The show featured dolphins, sea lions
and other sea life. When the show ended, the people
looked for comfortable places to sit and watch the
fireworks display. The fireworks display was
scheduled for ten o'clock. Two cannons were rolled
behind a large wire frame. Dr. Cruz walked across the
field to the podium.

 "I hope everyone is enjoying the carnival. I know it's
unusual for Polaris to have a carnival more than once
a year. However, this is a special occasion. This is
Polaris Town's tenth anniversary. So, what better way
to celebrate? Instead of firing the cannons first as
tradition would have us too, we are going to start the
fireworks first. Then at ten thirty, the cannons will be
fired. You will witness a very special life-like
fireworks display. This display will honor Polaris
Town. So sit back and enjoy yourselves."

 The traditional fireworks began. The night sky was
brilliant. Giant flowers, ribbons and whistling balls lit

up the sky. Everyone waited impatiently for ten thirty. They all wanted to see the Polaris Town's special fireworks display.

"I wonder what Dad is up too." Nick questioned. "This special event is a cover up and I know it."

"Well, what can we do about it, but sit and watch?" Reggie frowned.

 People would talk about the fireworks show, they'd see at ten thirty for weeks. Simultaneously, the cannons fired. A huge flag appeared whistling America the Beautiful. A giant rocket burst through the flag, leaving a trail of flames behind. The crowd was ecstatic. Long after the flag disappeared, they could still see the rocket. Other fireworks filled the night sky. The wire frame lit up with a lovely display commemorating Polaris' tenth anniversary. It was a spectacle worth seeing. The crowd *oohed* and *aahed* for nearly ten minutes. Dr. Cruz approached the podium at the end of the show.

 "The model rocket will come down some time tomorrow. The child, who finds it and returns it, will receive a five hundred dollar shopping spree at Polaris Mall."

The children applauded wildly, everyone except Nick.

"Model rocket my ass. Why would Polaris cover up a launch? It's not that unusual. One of Polaris' jobs is to send up the Nebulas for experimentation. There has got to be more to it."

Tracey Spencer walked over to the Explorers. "Hey Nick, your Dad really knows how to put on a fireworks show. It was amazing!"

"Not half as amazing as you babe." Max grinned.

"The rocket seemed so real!" Tracey gestured a rocket taking off. "If the fireworks hadn't been so far away, I would have sworn it was a real rocket. I bet they have a big write up on this in the Polaris Gazette. I can see the headlines. Polaris Town celebrates its tenth anniversary with a Fireworks Extravaganza!"

"This has been a night to remember," Tia interrupted.

"Well, what do we do now?" Angie Faye yawned.

"I'm hungry. Let's get something to eat before we go home." The Explorers hadn't eaten since lunch. The excitement of the carnival had died down and their stomachs were starting to complain.

"What do you mean before we go home? It's only eleven o'clock." Tracey frowned. "We have one more hour before the carnival ends. Let's have some fun. It'll be July before Polaris Town has another carnival. That's a long time to wait."

"Polaris Labs will be closed again tomorrow and so will school," Nick thought. "I'll enjoy tonight and find out what's going on Wednesday."

It took five shots for Adam to win a large black and white Panda. He and Pam played a few more games before heading home. The temperature dropped suddenly. Pam wished she had worn a sweater. The digital sign on Polaris Mall flashed; fifty-five degrees. Adam put the key in the ignition. Instantly the car purred to life.

"The car will be warm in a few minutes," he told Pam. "The temperature sure dropped fast."

They drove down the long dark highway towards Adam's townhouse. Clouds began to form. They soon covered the night sky. Pam was feeling restless again. The warm car and soft music from the radio didn't help. She quickly attributed it to fatigue. She couldn't wait to relax on the couch and drink a glass of wine. Adam pulled into his driveway.

"For the next twenty four hours, there will be no phone calls or visitors. It will be just you and I." He smiled, reaching into his pocket. He felt a small box. The soft cotton inside kept the ring from shaking. Adam smiled once again and closed the door behind him.

Chapter 4—DESTINATION EARTHSTAR

The halls of Polaris Laboratories were dark and almost deserted. One lone figure stood behind a stone pillar glancing around the restricted area. The tall man dressed in dark clothing hurried down the hall towards the computer room. The dark room soon glowed from the light of the computer. A male hand typed meticulously at the keyboard. The computer whirred to life with a series of beeps and clicks. The access codes were entered accurately. Earthstar's design flashed across the screen. The computer was instructed to locate and enhance the mechanical portion of the schematic diagram. One stroke of the key and a red space marked telemeter was magnified twice its original size. He entered the code for the main computer and instructed it to falsify all information sent back to the computer from the telemetry device.

He then instructed the computer to relay this information to all other computers involved in The Secret Under The Rainbow Project. His final task was to change the access codes, so that no one else could retrieve information about the alterations. The computer flashed the words lock out, three times. The shadowy figure quietly walked down the hall and exited the building. Polaris Labs were once again quiet and deserted.

The elevator doors of Polaris Guest Hotel slid open. A black glove touched P-1. The elevator began its ascension. The clock in the elevator read; four fifteen a.m. The sound of a bell announced the elevator's arrival. The halls were silent with the exception of the figure's spasmodic breathing. The sound of his footsteps echoed throughout the hall. He pushed the key into the lock and prayed when it clicked.

Penthouse level one was occupied by three of Dr. Cruz's guests. Tipping across the carpet, he entered his room and breathed a sigh of relief. The bed seemed to have an immediate calming effect on him. He closed his eyes and smiled a devious smile. A few seconds later, he was asleep.

Adam dragged himself into the shower. They had a long day ahead of them. Pam was in the kitchen preparing breakfast. She was nervous about meeting Adam's family. It would take six and a half hours to drive to his parent's house. Pam had taken Poseidon to the kennel and the neighborhood association had been informed about their trip. Adam let the car run for a few minutes, and then returned to the house for their jackets. The temperature was forty-nine and the wind was out of the north. Pam shivered. Her stomach felt queasy. Adam assured her it was just anxiety. They pulled out of the driveway and began their journey.

Adam's family lived forty-nine miles from the Gulf Coast. He hoped they would have time to go fishing. He was practically raised on a boat. He entitled one of his scariest memories, The Great Storm. It happened when he was nine years old. It was time for the Stanton men to take their annual three-generation excursion. The men would spend one week fishing, swimming and telling ghost stories. Somehow, they managed to sleep through a hurricane warning. Their boat was destroyed, Adam was injured and they barely survived. The memory was still burning in his mind when they reached his parent's house.

The Brain converted a walk-in closet into his private computer room. The room was dark and silent with the exception of a blinking light and a constant beep from the computer. Someone was being moved but the sound and light went unnoticed. The Nebula II lifted off Tuesday morning at four. The scheduled launching had been moved ahead because of approaching bad weather.

Nick called Reggie at twelve p.m.

"What are we gonna do today? We can't snoop around Polaris. My Dad has been there since last night. Did you see the Nebula II, this morning?"

"Yeah," Reggie yawned.

"All of the Explorers have plans today except us." Reggie complained. "I hate to say it but I'm looking forward to school tomorrow."

"Yeah, I know what you mean," Nick groaned.

"Hey, I know!" Reggie said excitedly. "Let's look for that rocket." Nick groaned. But, Reggie knew how to win Nick over. "Hey, if we find it, we could buy more supplies for the rover. We might also find out a little more about what Polaris is up to." That was enough to convince Nick to go rocket hunting. They searched for the rocket for several hours.

"There was never a model rocket," Nick complained. "Let's go to the mall. We can get something to eat and check out the pet store." The pet store was crowded. Several girls giggled and waved at Reggie. Nick was always interested in finding something odd to go in his fish tank. The manager promised to have new species by the end of the week.

"I don't feel like eating junk food. Let's eat at the Canis Canteen." Reggie suggested. The Canis Canteen was divided into two sections. The Canis Major was the main restaurant. It was decorated with crystal chandeliers, shaped like the constellation the restaurant was named for. Soft music flowed through the intercom. The setting was classy yet casual. Canis Minor was generally occupied by teens. Reggie suggested they eat in Canis Major. Nick soon understood why. Tia Quartz and her father Ryan were dining a few feet away. Reggie requested a table near the Quartz's. Tia introduced her father to the guys.

"Did you hear about The Brain?" She asked.

"What about him?" They asked.

"The radio announcer said he found the model rocket at six, this morning. Isn't that great?"

"So, there was a rocket," Reggie taunted.

Life was back to normal Wednesday morning. School began at seven fifteen. Polaris' employees were back from their brief vacation. Pam and Adam were exhausted. They had just returned to Enich Hills that morning. They decided to rest and be late for work. Polaris could do without them until noon.

Polaris High's cafeteria was always crowded and noisy. The cafeteria was popular because the students chose the meals. Nick, Reggie and Mike, a new pledge for The Explorers Club were seated in the middle of the cafeteria. Max joined the group.

"Has anyone seen The Brain today? He wasn't in chemistry class. And we all know *He* doesn't miss class for anything."

"He's probably out shopping with the prize money." Mike swallowed.

"Some guys have all the luck."

"This is Mike Shannon." Reggie said to Max. Mike and the other pledges would be introduced to the Explorers later that night. Their initiation and mock trial would begin at dusk.

"Hi Mike." Max shook hands with Mike. "No offense man, but what the hell are you?"

"None taken," Mike smiled. Mike's skin was brown. He had green eyes and long wavy black hair.

"My father is part Indian and white. My mother is part black. Her mother is from India. So, I guess you'd call me a mutt."

Everyone laughed. "I like him," Max said. "What's your specialty?"

"This guy is an electronics wizard." Reggie interrupted. "That's why I chose him as a pledge."

The bell rang. The cafeteria cleared out in less than ten minutes. "Don't forget to remind everyone about the meeting, tonight." Nick yelled.

The Artec had successfully taken off on Labor Day. The navigator glanced at his watch, twelve forty-five. Fifteen minutes ahead of schedule. The Artec was one of the few older rockets still in existence. It was generally used for small trips around the Earth or to gather samples from the moon. It took a lot of work to prepare the Artec for a trip to Earthstar.

Polaris Town came into existence for one purpose, to build and oversee The Secret Under The Rainbow Project. The majority of the I.S.S.A workers didn't know what became of their ideas or the projects they built. The Rainbow Project was so secret, different pieces were manufactured in different I.S.S.A towns. All towns were instructed to add restricted rainbow areas. The final stage of Earthstar was too important to be discovered until they were ready for the public to know.

The Artec moved into docking position. As the rocket locked into place, Earthstar shifted. The crew felt a jolt. It was like a small tremor and just like insignificant tremors; it was overlooked.

On another rocket less than twenty minutes away. A young boy sat twiddling his thumbs. "How can I let them know? They'll expect me to do something, but what?" A million questions went through the young man's mind. He knew his parents would never deliberately hurt him. They were here too. So, it couldn't be that bad. He felt like part of a conspiracy. "I've betrayed my friends and most of all myself."

The Nebula II was the fastest mode of space travel ever designed. The Artec at top speed took four days to reach Earthstar. The Nebula II was traveling at cruise speed. If the need arrived, Nebula II could reach Earthstar in six hours. The navigator of the Nebula II called the dock masters.

"Nebula II will be ready to dock in twenty minutes. Please have the tram ready to pick up the Chandler and Bradford families."

The Brain realized he and his mother were not alone in their abduction. Two seats over, Toby Chandler huddled against the window. His parents were seated behind him. Why weren't his parents trying to console him? His father's voice came over the intercom.

"We'll be docking in ten minutes. I know the docking will be smooth but for precaution sake, buckle up."

Admiral Robert Bradford was proud to be part of the Polaris Team. He took his job very seriously.

Navigation was not easy but he loved it. His family were about to join the Earthstar community. He was quite proud of this. Charles would actually attend school in outer space. Living and communicating with aliens was something most people only dreamed about. Only the best suited families would be chosen to live on Earthstar. This society would advance a lot faster and further than Polaris.

"Charles may be angry with me now, but someday he will thank me."

"Something's wrong." The assistant navigator gasped. "We're headed into the planetoid's living sectors, not the docking areas."

"How can that be?" Admiral Bradford's calculations were always correct. "We were headed directly for dock three, twenty minutes ago. What Happened?"

"Look," his assistant pointed. "The computers are still set at their original destinations. Nothing has changed."

But something had changed.

"Has Earthstar altered her orbit? Nebula II must have a malfunction in the guidance system. We'll have to dock manually." Admiral Bradford was confused.

Nebula II entered a long docking tunnel. Curved squiggly lights encircled the inside of the tunnel. The Nebula II landed smoothly.

Brain looked out the window. He couldn't see anything. The windows were covered with a thick mist. The doors of Nebula II slid open. A tall man was waiting for them.

"Hi, I'm professor Norvin." He spoke with a strange accent. Brain couldn't figure out what kind of accent the man had. The strange man had black glossy hair with streaks of gray and gold on the sides. Brain wasn't sure if he imagined it or if the man really did have familiar eyes.

"Don't be sad," the man said. "Some of your friends are already here. Others will join you. I think you will find your new homes very interesting. The schools are light years ahead of any school or university, you could attend on Earth. Everything is automated. As soon as your belongings are loaded on the tram you may proceed to your new homes." The tram was similar to an aerodynamic subway train, only shorter. "The trams glides on air, therefore we don't need rails."

Professor Norvin smiled. His smile was unnatural and made the boys uncomfortable.
The Brain touched his father's shoulders.

"Dad, whose going to take the Nebula II back to Earth?"

"I am son. I'll leave tomorrow night. Navigating the Nebulas is still my job. I'll travel back and forth. We'll still have plenty of time to spend together."

The tram was empty. "Who's driving this thing?" Toby questioned.

"It's automated. Remember everything is automated." Professor Norvin sounded frustrated. They boarded the tram quietly. Two minutes later, they were riding inside Earthstar.

Earthstar was a world within a mechanical bubble. There were fountains, manicured lawns, flowers and parks. The buildings were a soft metallic gray and bronze. The lighting was artificial and there was no glare from the buildings. Overhead was a blue sky with fluffy white clouds. The sound of chirping birds filled the air.

Toby whispered to The Brain. "I hear birds but I don't see them."

"Now that you mention it, I don't see any animals." The Brain tapped Professor Norvin on the shoulder.

"Do you have any animals here?"

"Oh yes, Professor Damni has lots of them in the labs."

The children watched out the windows. The streets were empty and so were the parks. "I don't think Earthstar is everything it's cracked up to be." Toby whispered. "Maybe the people here are human computers."
The tram stopped on a narrow metallic street. The automatic sidewalks took them down the street until they reached a small cove. The houses were identical.

There was one small difference, the strange drawings that illuminated the right side of each door.

Professor Norvin handed each family a shiny disc. These discs carry information about you and contain your clearance codes. The Bradford's house was in the center of the cove. The Chandler's house was near the end of the cove. Admiral Bradford inserted the silver disc into a small glass receptacle. *Bradford family identification confirmed. You may enter the premises.* The words flashed across the door in a brilliant white light. The metallic doors slid quietly apart. The Brain looked back. The Chandlers were headed towards their new home.

The house was too clean. The Brain touched a metal bar. No fingerprints appeared. He tried numerous times but he could not smear the surface. The living room had strange shaped furniture. The tables and floors were made of the same metal the house and bar were made of. The couch, loveseat and chair were covered in a silvery material with red and blue specks. The material felt soft when he touched it. The rugs and carpet were identical to the material on the furniture. A spinning disc controlled the recessed lights. A metallic table and chair set glistened in the kitchen. The metal surface was warm.

"Where's the stove and refrigerator?" Mrs. Bradford asked.

"Things operate a little different here." Her husband explained, pointing to a panel on the wall. It had twenty small colored lights and a little door which opened diagonally. He pointed to an information packet on the table.

"This will explain everything about the house."
Admiral Bradford led his family to the escalators.

"Charles, the escalators will take you to your room
downstairs. All houses are entered upstairs. The
remainder of the house is underground. If anything
ever goes wrong, get to the lowest floor. You'll have
a better chance of survival. Now let's talk about
happier things."

 The escalators moved slowly. There were four rooms
and three bedrooms downstairs. The halls were
rounded like the tunnels. The same squiggly lights
lined the walls. The first room was his parents'
bedroom. It was large and shaped like an octagon. A
small-lighted panel similar to the one in the kitchen
was on the wall. The room was decorated with
glowing filaments that danced in a make believe
breeze.

"Where's the bed?" The Brain asked.

"The buttons on the wall activates the bed, dresser,
closet and lamps. This blue button opens the door to
the bathroom." Admiral Bradford pushed the button
and a section of the metal wall slid open.

 The bathroom contained a sink, sunken tub and the
strangest toilet they'd ever seen. The toilet looked
like a seat on the spaceship rides at Polaris' carnival.
 The next room was the game room. There was a
game similar to billiards. The table was crystal. The
balls were holographic. They were moved with a light
from a small holographic pen attached to the end of

the table. The other games were so strange that The Brain quickly lost interest.

The Bradford's moved through the other bedrooms quickly. The last room was the atrium. It was decorated with laser lights. There was a small blue pool with multicolored fish, gold stones and a waterfall.

"Now it's time for you to get ready for school, young man." Admiral Bradford pushed a yellow button in The Brain's room. The doors slid apart revealing a closet full of golden metallic jumpsuits. "This is what everyone here wears." The Brain was not impressed. "The tram will be here in twenty minutes, so get dressed." Admiral Bradford handed his son a jumpsuit.

"But Dad it's almost two o'clock," The Brain whined.

"Schools here start at one p.m. and end at seven thirty. They like the idea of students going to bed with their lessons on their minds. The good thing about this is you don't have to get up early in the mornings."

The Brain dressed quickly. "I feel like a geek. I wonder if Toby we'll be there." Toby was standing on the corner waiting for the tram. He was constantly tugging at the collar of the jumpsuit. "Nerd city," he said when he saw The Brain.

The tram stopped in front of the school. They placed their discs into a brass slot. It instructed them on proper conduct and then directed them to class. The clock in the hall had three o'clock. "At least we only have four hours left," Toby sighed. They entered a small auditorium. Seventy seats were arranged in a semi-circle. Only twenty eight seats were occupied. The teacher told them to take a seat. She looked like any other teacher except for her eyes. She had unusually small octagon shaped eyes. Her accent was identical to Professor Norvin's. The room shifted and Toby stumbled down the stairs. The Brain held onto the transparent railing. Toby sat beside a red-haired boy with freckles. He immediately recognized him.

"Ricky Schaeffer," He exclaimed a little too loudly. "Are the Harrison's here too?"

"Yes, I have a list of the other Polaris families that are coming." Ricky stated.

"How long are they gonna keep us here?" The Brain whispered.

"Forever!" Ricky leaned closer to the other boys. "They are going to mate us with the alien families."

"Alien families," Toby gasped.

"Yes," Ricky nodded.

 Ricky leaned closer. "They intend to mate us with the Caniculiens and start a new race of super beings. These new beings will be smarter, stronger and live longer than their predecessors."
"Where are the aliens now?" Toby asked.

They are all around you. Ricky wrote his answer on a golden tablet. The teacher was looking at him, so he continued to write his response.

The teacher, the man who met you at the docks and half of the students are Caniculiens. Toby and The Brain realized that studies weren't the only thing to learn at school. The day ended too quickly for the boys. There was so much they needed to find out. The Brain knew he had to find a way to contact the Explorers. He had to warn them. He didn't want to be part of the I.S.S.A's experiments. They had to find a way to get into the school's labs and make a disc to send to the Explorers. Ricky told them Earthstar is heavily guarded and sneaking out is impossible.

Chapter 5—STRANGE OCCURRENCES

Nick was sleeping peacefully when the phone rang. "This had better be important," he said.

"Get dressed and meet me at the big tree near Brain's house." A dial tone hummed in Nick's ear. He was sure the voice belonged to Reggie.

Nick dressed quickly. "Man, I hope this is worth my getting up for." He knew that Reggie wouldn't call at three in the morning, unless it was important. Reggie was leaning against the large Oak tree.

"Let's go," he whispered to Nick. They crossed the street, climbed a wooden fence and then jumped into Brain's backyard. The Bradford's house was dark. A rope ladder The Brain used to climb out his window, twisted in the wind. They could see the light from the computer glowing in the room. The boys climbed the ladder and entered The Brain's room. It was silent, with the exception of an occasional beep from The

Brain's computer. Ironically, the computer was sending The Brain a message of his own abduction. Nick erased the Explorer's programs from the computer. He knew Polaris would soon come to clear out the house. "That's why they lied, claiming The Brain found the model rocket. It was to cover up his disappearance, temporarily."

"If I know The Brain," Reggie yawned. "He'll try to get a message to us. So we'll have to tell the Explorers to keep their eyes open."

"What about the pledges?" Nick asked.

"Well, they are almost Explorers and we're gonna need their help."

They decided to tell the Explorers to skip school the next day. They realized they couldn't help The Brain until he contacted them. Sadly, the two friends headed home.

The Bradford family spent the day learning about their new surroundings. The Brain couldn't wait to get to school. His parents were delighted with his enthusiasm. In the science lab, the students were encouraged to create projects of their own. Toby, Ricky and The Brain sat together. Stanley Harrison and his twin sister Stacey were also in the science lab.

"Shouldn't we ask them to help?" Toby asked.

"NO!" Ricky whispered. "They maybe from Polaris Town but they are loyal to the system. Well at least Stanley is. I am not so sure about Stacey. She's very popular here and I don't trust her."

The Brain pointed to a strange machine. "Show me how to record the message." They recorded a message explaining everything Ricky told them. The disc was the size of a quarter. It would easily fit between the clips on the back of the Explorers' pin. The only problem they could foresee was the Explorers not being capable of making a device to play it on. But they had to have faith in the Explorers.

The boys decided to spend the night with The Brain. Admiral Bradford was leaving Earthstar later that night. They would hide the Explorers' club pin in the Nebula's trash compartment. School ended thirty minutes later than usual. The tram had come and gone. The school called for a special tram to take the students home. The tram arrived five minutes later.

Toby's parents were thrilled the boys were spending the night together. Toby didn't have many friends in Polaris Town. Most of his time was spent building robots. Mrs. Bradford cooked glazed ham, macaroni and cheese, yams and green peas for dinner. The meal was delicious. After dinner, Ricky taught the boys to play the strange billiard game. They played quietly while Admiral Bradford took a nap. Once the house was quiet, it was time to discuss their strategy. Secretly sneaking the pin into the trash compartment would take careful planning.

A mini tram took them to the docking areas. Mrs. Bradford felt she would be lost in this new world without her husband. Admiral Bradford tried to explain how much easier it would be for them to live on Earthstar. The Brain took advantage of his father trying to comfort his mother. "Dad, can I show the guys the helm of the Nebula II." His father answered yes out of guilt.

The boys climbed aboard the Nebula II. Toby stood guard while The Brain removed the screws from the trash compartment. The cordless screwdriver, Toby had taken from his father's toolbox did the job immediately.

"Hurry up," Toby whispered. "Your father is standing at the bottom of the steps." They hid the pin in the back of a small compartment behind the trash shoot.

"Your father is coming," Toby panicked.

"It's alright. I am putting in the last two screws." The Brain stood up, pretending to explain the star charts.

"My son is going to be a navigator someday," his father thought. Toby relaxed and gave a sigh of relief. The Brain hugged his father and told him goodbye.

The tram ride home seemed very long. The Bradford's were both sad and frightened. They felt as if they were being devoured by this new world. Mrs. Bradford tried to smile reassuringly. The other families were here but they were complete. She and her son were alone. The boys tried watching TV. All of the shows were based on education and human and alien interactions. Toby turned off the TV. Ricky connected The Brain's video game to the TV.

"Now this is entertainment!" Ricky laughed.

"Never leave this game connected. They are illegal here. The teachers say video games make us slow and ignorant."

The wind was gusting to twenty five miles an hour. Clouds threatened to burst at any minute. Nick was glad school had ended for the week. As he turned the corner towards home, a raindrop hit his head. "Not yet," he thought. "Let me make it home first." He walked at a steady pace. Two more raindrops landed on his forehead. The drops became larger and fell faster. Nick picked up the pace and so did the rain.

His mother stood in the window watching for him. Nick was soaking wet. The rain was cold and the temperature was dropping. "Get out of those wet clothes and take a shower. I'll make some tea," his mother comforted.

Nick was covered in soap when the lights went out. He finished his shower and put on a blue robe. He felt his way to his bedroom door. " Mom," he yelled. She handed him a flashlight. Tying his robe tighter, he followed her downstairs. They sat on the couch, sipping tea and watching the storm.

"When is Dad coming home?" Nick asked.

"The Nebula II is supposed to return at nine tonight. I'm sure your father will be very late." She sighed.

Nick finished his tea. "I think I'll turn in early tonight."

"I know this weather is perfect for sleeping but what about dinner?" Mrs. Cruz asked.

"I guess we could eat sandwiches." Nick said stumbling to the kitchen. Nick fixed two sandwiches and ran up to his room. The static in the phone was horrible. He could not tell whether the phone was ringing or not. After finishing the two sandwiches, he decided to sneak out of the house.

Mrs. Cruz realized Nick was up to something. "He's young; he should enjoy it while he can. If you're leaving, be careful." Nick smiled.

His mother was great. She would worry about him being out in the storm. But, she knew if he was determined to do something, nothing could stop him. Nick walked down the slippery streets. He thought about taking a short cut. However, in the downpour it would probably be too dangerous. Lightning flashed across the sky. The lightning branched out like limbs on a tree. Nick loved lightning. Storms fascinated him. Although he was wearing a raincoat, the wind was blowing so wildly that he got soaked. He knocked on Reggie's window. This was one time, he was happy Reggie's window faced the front of the house. Reggie grabbed his raincoat. Nick had plans for them and that meant getting wet.

They entered Polaris Labs at eight o'clock. Nick called his father to get permission to watch the landing. The backup generator pulled the elevator slowly towards the tower. The elevator whined loudly.

"Why are we here?" Reggie asked. Nick told him about the VIP's staying at Polaris Guest Hotel. While they were having dinner with his father, they seemed very excited about the return of Nebula II. The tower was alive with activity. The boys hung around until the Nebula II landed. Sneaking into the briefing room proved to be very easy.

"Brain's Dad is still the navigator! How could they be so stupid?" Reggie puzzled.

"No one's here to see him. Dad thinks we're in the tower." Nick explained.

The meeting was informal. Nothing was said to help the boys. They decided to walk to the landing strip. They were standing at the base of the Nebula II, when Dr. Cruz spotted them. "I thought you boys were in the tower."

"We wanted to look at her before going home." Nick lied.

"Well, since you are here, you can help me. Look in the storage compartment of the helm and bring me the flight records. I'll be in my office. I'll leave clearance for you two at the desk," he said walking away. They climbed the slippery steps, which led to the helm's door. The rain showed no signs of stopping. The temperature inside the Nebula II was fifty eight degrees. The boys began to shiver. They sat in the navigator's and his assistant's seats.

"I can just see myself flying this baby," Nick said. Reggie picked up a tissue, blew his nose and tossed the tissue in the trash chute.

"Let's go Nick, we've got the files. I'm cold and wet. We can look for clues tomorrow."

After taking the flight records to Dr. Cruz, they headed home. Something whooshed overhead.

"Look," Reggie exclaimed. "Ball lightning! I thought it was just a myth!" Huge blue and white balls of light zipped above them.

"This is getting rough. We'd better hurry home." Reggie was right. A few minutes later, a siren wailed loudly. The boys rushed home.

Saturday morning, it was still raining. Nick wanted to go to Polaris Labs with his father. Dr. Cruz was very nonchalant. He did not need Nick disturbing him. Saturday and Sunday passed uneventful. It had rained both days. The weatherman said, he wasn't sure when the rain would stop.

School was canceled both Monday and Tuesday because of the rain and power outages. Flash floods were inevitable. Rivers and creeks began to overflow. Volunteers filled sand bags and placed them along the banks of the rivers. The streets of Polaris Town looked like a giant wading pool. Schools were canceled for the week. The news advised everyone to stay at home. The rain finally stopped, Thursday night. The waters would soon begin to subside. Children waded in the waters. To them, it was just another vacation. The temperature rose to seventy nine degrees. It was going to be a beautiful Friday. The waters were subsiding but the ground was still soggy. People were taking advantage of the sunny day. Friday night, the temperatures plummeted to thirty five degrees.

Saturday morning, the weatherman said the temperature would reach seventy degrees. But, the temperature continued to drop. It stopped at twenty three degrees. The weather was strange. People all around the world were focusing their attention on the nation's strange weather.

 Schools reopened the following Tuesday. The weather was still cold. None of the regular subjects were taught. Everyone was still focusing on the unusual weather. Places normally hot were now cold. Alaska had a temperature of eighty eight. Hawaii was at thirty degrees. Glaciers melted, volcanoes cooled, no one could explain what or why this was happening.

 Everyone had theories but no one had the answers. The United Nations called for an emergency meeting. Dr. Cruz and other scientists flew to New York for the meeting. Two days later, the newspapers reported the world's scientists had solved the weather problems. No one believed it but in less than a week, the weather was back to normal. Life went on as usual. People quickly forgot about the freaky weather.

"Dr. Cruz," a voice over the intercom called. "Please come to the rainbow conference room." Dr. Cruz, Dr. Quartz, Dr. Wensworth and Professor Donovan were seated around a large conference table. Admiral Robert Bradford informed them of the computer malfunctions on board the Nebula II.

"We checked the Nebula II and found nothing wrong. I realize you are our best navigator," Dr. Quartz said. "But, even the best can make mistakes." Admiral Bradford tried to argue but decided it was useless. He left the conference disappointed.

"I've made that trip to many times. I could fly it blindfolded. Just because they didn't find the glitch, doesn't mean I'm incompetent." He was determined to find the problem. The man responsible for cleaning the Nebulas was home with the flu. The strange weather had gotten the best of him. Dr. Cruz needed to replace him. On such short notice, it would be hard to find someone he could trust. He decided to get Nick and one of his friends to clean the Nebula II. First, he would make sure no evidence of the passengers was left behind.

Nick was not exactly thrilled about playing janitor for the day. Why couldn't his Dad ever trust him to do important jobs? He asked Reggie to help him. Reggie vacuumed, while Nick cleaned the seats. Reggie washed the windows on the right side of the Nebula II. Nick took care of the left. They felt relieved when they finally reached the helm.

"We're almost finished," Nick groaned. He opened the trash compartment and removed the trash bags. The replacement bags were stored in a little compartment inside the panel below the trash shoot. He removed the screws and flipped open the small door. He pulled out a trash bag and closed the door. Reggie replaced the screws, while Nick put the trash bag in place. They exhaustedly crawled down the steps.

"We're finished Dad," Nick complained. "Can we go now?" Dr. Cruz nodded and went to inspect their work. He knew the boys had done a good job but his perfectionism forced him to check behind them. Everything was perfect. He caught up with the boys in the corridor. He surprised them by promising to do a favor for them. They were grateful for this. They weren't sure what type of help they would need to save The Brain.

During lunch break, the students were allowed to eat outside. Toby, The Brain and Ricky sat under a strange squiggly tree with weird shaped leaves. The leaves were bright red. "What kind of a tree is this?" Toby asked. "This is a Rhodafern. It's supposed to bring good luck." Ricky broke off a small twig. Red sap poured from the tree. "It's said if it bleeds for you, you'll have good luck."
The Brain swallowed hard. "I hope they found it."

"You mean you hope no one else found it." Toby smirked. The lunch break ended and it was back to class for the boys.

On the way home, The Brain gave Toby and Ricky an Explorers' pin. "I am officially accepting you as new members of The Explorers Club. All in favor state I." The Brain stood up and said I. "The motion has been made and approved. You are now Explorers." Toby's dream had come true. It didn't happen in Polaris Town but it still happened. To him, it was like Christmas had come early. Toby was so happy. He had to fight a tear forming in his eye. He had just become an Explorer. He didn't want to look like a wimp. It was too bad he couldn't tell his parents. They would be so proud of him.

The next day proved to be very strange. The Brain's body felt like he had been exercising for hours. His heart rate increased. He was tired and dragging. His legs felt as though he was wearing weighted boots. " Mom," he called slowly. "I'm so tired. I don't think I can make it to school this evening." Mrs. Bradford slowly entered the room.

"Perhaps we have a virus. I'll fix us a bowl of cereal and a glass of orange juice. Maybe, the sugar will give us some energy." Little did they know, people everywhere on Earthstar were dragging and feeling tired.

After breakfast, The Brain forced himself to take a shower. It took a lot of energy and willpower to enter the bathroom. The house shook. "I must really be losing it," he thought. Although the Bradford's were still dragging, they had gained a greater amount of energy by twelve o'clock. The Brain decided he would go to school.

There weren't very many students at school. The school closed early. Toby, Ricky and The Brain waited for the tram under the Rhodafern. Toby broke off a twig. Nothing happened. "Look," he told The Brain. They could see the red sap. The sap had congealed. "It looks like a giant blood clot," Toby gasped. The temperature was starting to drop.

"Ricky, I thought you said the temperature here was consistent," Toby stated.

"Efficiency doesn't last forever. Even the most perfect world has its flaws." The Brain said.

The tram arrived late. It moved slower than usual, but no one complained. Everyone was too tired.
In the darkness of space, Earthstar fell victim to a number of spasmodic jerks. Then quietly and gently, Earthstar tilted towards Earth's magnetic poles. The

lights of Earthstar shimmered. Short periods of light and darkness flashed. To its inhabitants, it simply looked like clouds passing over the sun. Earthstar bowed her head. She quietly slipped out of her original orbit and into a shorter orbit.

Toby and The Brain walked towards their homes. Toby saw something glowing near a tree. He picked it up. It was a crystalline rock, a rock that had somehow gained the power of illumination. Something was wrong and no one really seemed to notice. The Explorers had to find their message. "If they don't," he said aloud. "We're doomed!"

Good evening and welcome to another edition of the six o' clock eye witness news. In world news today, a giant waterspout hit the Maldives Islands off the coast of India. Male', its capital was completely destroyed. The death toll is unknown. There has been no further communication with the islands.

Temperatures in Saudi Arabia got so hot, the Red Sea was said to have literally boiled. The people of Yemen claimed to have caught boiled fish near the Gulf of Aden. Volcanoes erupted around the globe, today. Paricutin, Mexico, Italy, Hawaii, Russia and even here at home in the good ole U.S. of A. Mount Saint Helens is once again spewing the spittle of hell. We'll continue with the world news after this commercial break."

The Explorers club had finally gotten a portable TV. "The news is always "A" typical, in other words all bad," Tia said.

The Explorers hadn't heard anything from The Brain. They had no clues and no idea where to start looking. The news spoke of mudslides in South America, Tidal waves in Japan and floods and hurricanes in Cuba and Jamaica. The end of the news report was strange but interesting.

"In other news, glaciers have been melting at a phenomenal rate. The icebergs formed from chunks of ice breaking off the glaciers have been ramming ships in the nearby seas. Our final story is a strange one. We've received reports from pet owners and zoos all over the world. It seems the animals are becoming very temperamental. The dogs are becoming more aggressive. Horses are pacing nervously and get this; the fish are actually leaving the waters. Well, that's our news for now. I'm Max Shlenker, goodnight."

"It seems as though the natural disasters are increasing," Tia said. "Wouldn't it be great to go to the zoo outside of Polaris Town and see if the animals really are acting freaky?"

"I wonder if the United Nations will try to solve this problem," Lenny laughed.

"My Mom was searching my room last night," Angie Faye laughed. "She was looking for my cigarettes. She knows I smoke. She just hasn't been able to prove it. So I just took the pack and hid it in the fake bottom of my trashcan. She'll never find them. I mean she may as well give up."

"That's it," Nick yelled. "Reggie, how could we have been so damned ignorant?"

"What the hell are you talking about Nick?" Reggie looked confused.

"The secret trash compartment. I even changed the trash bags."

"I just didn't think. If The Brain was going to try to get in touch with us, he would have left a message in the small compartment. We've got to find a way to get back into the Nebula II."

"What if?" Tia said fidgeting with her hair. "What if all the weird weather and natural disasters and the behavior of the animals had something to do with The Brain's abduction?"

"Well," Lenny said. "If it does then we're all in a heap of shit. You know, a major hellhole. Nick, if the tower is empty and you can keep your father busy; we could sneak aboard the Nebula II and check the storage compartment."

Nick called his father's office. "Dad, I'm doing a project for school and I'm really confused. I need your help. I know that you are busy… "

"I am never too busy to help you with your school work," his father interrupted. "Come to my office. I'll leave a temporary pass at the guard's desk." Step one was complete.

Nick had access. He would give the pass to Reggie, then Reggie could check out the computer systems. While Reggie was busy learning new information, Lenny and Tia could swing into action. They would sneak over the fence and board the Nebula II. Tia would stand guard.

The plan worked perfect. Lenny found The Brain's Explorers' pin with the disc attached. Now, all the Explorers had to do was to invent a machine to play it on. Reggie and Angie Faye were perfect for this job. Reggie's skills with electronics and Angie Faye's skill with robotics would make the task a lot easier. Trying to build this machine would take a lot of time and energy. They needed a machine similar to a compact disc player only a lot smaller and more complex. Reggie told the Explorers the computer's system seemed to be normal.

"It will take The Brain to find an error in that system." Reggie and Angie Faye decided to spend all their extra time at the clubhouse working on the project. Tia and Max were in charge of getting the supplies Reggie and Angie Faye needed to build the machine.

Chapter 6—THE GYRO DISC

Pam turned the radio on. The music pacified her
while she drove. Sometimes, driving made her
nervous. She didn't understand how some people had
so much fun driving. The radio played loudly. "But
the dreams, I've seen lately. Keep on turning out and
turning out the same...." Pam sang along with the
radio. She loved the old songs.

The sun had gone down. It would be dark soon.
She'd had a very hectic day at work. "I can't wait to
get home and relax." Something flashed ahead of her.
"What's that?" Just over the horizon, a large round
ball appeared. It was like seeing a reflection of Earth
in a mirror. It disappeared as soon as it appeared.
"What the hell was that? I'm not that tired and I don't
exactly have a habit of seeing things. What's
happening?" She asked herself.

Pam pulled into her driveway then dialed the code on her garage door opener. The door slowly rose. She pulled into the double garage. Pam was preparing to enter the house, when she noticed a blue BMW parked beside her. It was not Adam's car. This was a new BMW. "It couldn't be," she thought. Pam quickly unlocked the door. "Adam," she called. Adam was in the kitchen eating a ham and Swiss cheese sandwich.

"How do you like our new car?" He asked.

"Our new car!" She looked confused. Adam handed Pam a small light blue box. She opened the box and gasped. The box contained a beautiful blue diamond engagement ring.

"Well," he said. "If you're gonna be my wife, take a bite of my sandwich. If not go ahead and slap me in the face." Pam took a big bite of the sandwich. Adam kissed her. "Now, you know why I wanted you to meet my family." Adam pulled Pam into the living room. "We'll call my family and tell them tonight. So, when do we tell your family?"

"Later, I'm hungry," Pam smiled. "What's for dinner?"

"Well, I thought we could have a nice quiet romantic dinner at home." Adam smiled. "I called that new restaurant, you liked so much."

"But, they don't deliver," she said.

"They do when you're paying them a king's ransom," he grinned. "You have time to soak in the tub and put on something sexy, sensational and yet comfortable. The caterers will be her by nine fifteen."

Pam filled the tub with bubble bath. The water splashed loudly in the tub. She was so happy. She'd never imagined Adam was ready for marriage. She wondered how her family would react. "I wish everyone could love Adam as much I do." She knew in her heart, she would marry Adam whether her family liked him or not.

Adam removed a statue from the coffee table. He replaced it with a light blue tablecloth. A small candelabrum was placed in the center of the table. Light blue candles with the words I love you and the date printed in gold were placed in the candelabrum. There was a candle for each year they had been together. Tonight was their fourth anniversary.

"There's no better way to celebrate an anniversary, than with a marriage proposal and acceptance. I wonder if Pam is as happy as I am." He placed four light blue roses in a crystal bud vase. A blue lace ribbon was neatly tied around the vase. An oversized anniversary card leaned against the vase. The caterers had been told to bring all the decorations in light blue and white. These were the colors Pam wore the night she and Adam met. He removed a light blue silk camisole with matching shorts and robe from a department store bag. He arranged them neatly on the bed. A larger bag was hidden in the closet. It contained a man's silk robe and lounging shorts.

The doorbell rang. The caterers set the table elegantly. The food was placed on blue serving carts. Adam was pleased. Everything looked and smelled

great. After the caterers left, he went into the
bedroom and changed clothes. Pam stood in front of
the mirror brushing her hair. When she entered the
bedroom, she was surprised to see the clothing lying
on the bed. The food's wonderful aroma drifted into
the bedroom. Her stomach growled noisily. Adam lit
the candles and called Pam. She was amazed at the
way he had decorated the table. Pam liked the idea of
being dressed like Adam. It was all so special. She
sat on the silk pillow and read the inscription on the
candles. "It's our fourth anniversary!" She had
forgotten.

 After dinner, Adam placed the engagement ring on
Pam's finger. The TV was set to automatically come
on during the late news. Malcolm Schwin stood in
front of the camera. Several residents of Enich Hills
and the surrounding areas reported seeing a large
round object in the sky. Many said it was like looking
at a giant model of Earth. The Air Force would like
us to put your minds at ease. What you saw was a
large blue weather balloon. The Air Force will be
doing several tests over the next few days.

"Adam!" Pam gasped. "I saw that on my way home
tonight. It was no weather balloon. It was too solid.
It was too real."

"You heard the news, sweetheart." He taunted.
"Now, let's go to bed. We have important business to
take of."

Pam awoke at two thirty, the next morning. She had
to be at work at seven A.M. She glanced at the clock
and then entered the bathroom. On her way back to
bed, she looked out the window. "The moon is

awfully bright." She thought. "Wait a minute, that's not the moon!" The Earth-like thing was back. "Adam," she yelled. He slowly crawled out of bed. They stood at the window together watching the thing glow.

"Weather balloons don't glow." Adam said.

"That's no weather balloon." Pam gasped.

Two weeks later, the sightings were being reported more and more frequently. Dr. Cruz finally realized something was wrong with Earthstar. The computers constantly claimed everything was normal. "The computers have to be malfunctioning because Earthstar should not be in Earth's orbit."

He called in his special computer team. They would work around the clock until they found and solved the problem. All other Polaris employees were told to stay home. They were told they were being rewarded for a job well done.

Friday evening, The Explorers Club gathered together. This was to be a very important meeting. Reggie and Angie Faye had completed a machine to play the disc. It was now time for the Explorers to hear what The Brain had to say.

"The sound won't be perfect." They told the others. "This disc is beyond our technology. We played the disc earlier. It will sound a little scratchy and faint. But, you will be able to understand what's happening. Please listen carefully. This is vital to The Brain's survival as well as our own!"

Reggie inserted the disc. Static sounded loudly. A high-pitched squeak sounded immediately after the static. Everyone covered his or her ears. The loud sound stopped and the static eased up a little. A strange sounding voice began to speak.

"This is Brain. I am on Earthstar. There are other people here too. Not just from Polaris, but from I.S.S.A towns around the globe. Three other Polaris families are scheduled to join us. The families are the Woodruffs, the Norwins and the Donovans. Not all of the Donovans, just Steffie and her Mom. Reggie and Max now that you know you are next on the list, please be careful Run away if you have too. We are all part of an experiment."

"They want to integrate humans and aliens called Caniculiens. They look just like us only their skin is a golden brown and their eyes are like long octagons. The experiment is to make a new generation of super beings; a smarter race that will live longer than its predecessors. Your parents already know they are next. They agreed to be part of this experiment. The next ship will leave Polaris in eight weeks. This place is a prison. They have guards everywhere. The Caniculien kids are just as angry and disgusted as we are."

"We attend a university of sorts. Everything is so advanced. It's all computerized and automated. Everyone has to be in their homes by ten o'clock. We cannot watch regular TV or play video games. Ricky said it is illegal. He sounded frightened when he said it."

"Remember Synacom 14? Well the Caniculiens invented it. We can't trust anyone. Making this gyro disc is risky. I knew you guys would find a way to play it. The building just shook. Something is wrong here. There are a lot of small tremors. They are becoming more and more frequent. My Dad's the best navigator that Polaris has. When we arrived here, the docking area was not in line with the Nebula II. Dad had to dock manually. Earthstar is slipping out of orbit. The computers say that everything is normal, but that's impossible."

"Explorers, I fear for our lives as well as yours. By the time you get this gyro disc, the situation will have worsened. I know, we are only kids but the future may depend on us. The adults will believe whatever the computers say. It's either a small undetectable malfunction or its sabotage. Do what you can and so will we. Remember, the future is in your hands."

Professor Norvin typed frantically at the keyboard. He had to send information to Polaris Labs. Canicula had little or no computer knowledge. Therefore, Polaris Labs were the main headquarters. He reported the abnormalities on Earthstar. He beseeched them to send technicians immediately. Polaris would get in touch with Canicula, they would both send technicians and Earthstar's problems would be solved. The screen went blank. "Ah," he thought. "The computer is sending my message."

Words appeared on his screen. He leaned closer to retrieve the message. Something was wrong. The message on the screen was from him. What could he do? The next Caniculien ship wasn't scheduled to arrive for six weeks. Polaris' ship would not arrive for another eight weeks.

The rainbow computer team had been working all night. The computers were broken down, rebuilt and the programs were checked over and over again. Dr. Cruz was summoned to the computer room. "We have found the problem." One member of the team said. "Someone reprogrammed the system. The information we've been receiving from the telemetry devices isn't accurate."

"Can't you do something about it?" Dr. Cruz questioned.

"No sir," the man replied. "Whoever did it knew all the access codes. They had no problem altering them. They also added a self-destruct system. If anybody tries to access the code, the entire system will blow. The only thing you can do is to find the culprit and get him or her to disarm the system."

Pam and Adam sat on the deck in her backyard. They discussed the sudden vacation from Polaris and the strange thing they had seen in the sky. Pam made a pitcher of lemonade. It was going to be another hot day.

"This would be a good day to open the pool," Pam hinted.

"All right," Adam smiled. "I'll get started. Why don't we have a pool party to celebrate our engagement?"

"That's a great idea," a voice from behind them said. They both turned around. Nick was standing outside the gate.

"Nick, what are you doing here? You're not supposed to leave Polaris Town." Pam complained.

"One question at a time," he said. "How about letting me in first." Adam opened the gate.

"I don't suppose you're here to help clean the pool." Adam grunted.

Nick laughed. "I can. But, I have more important things to discuss." Adam shook his head.

Nick patted him on the back. "First, let me congratulate you guys. Next, forgive me for intruding without permission. To answer your question, I hid in a laundry truck and thumbed the rest of the way. I am here to talk about Earthstar."

"What?" Pam interrupted.

"Earthstar!" Nick repeated.

"Let's get the pool cleaned first." Adam said. "Then you and Nick can talk." Pam turned on the radio and began to sing.

"Piece of newspaper at my feet," Pam sang happily. "Got our stories, old and new. Need someone to tell them to." The phone rang, temporarily interrupting their fun. Pam's sister called to say she was three months pregnant. Pam was going to be an aunt. She was so excited. She told her sister about the pool

party. "I'll have to call you back and give you a date."
Their conversation lasted fifteen minutes. Pam
prepared lunch while Adam and Nick finished the
pool. The three friends ate lunch on the deck. They
had sandwiches and lemonade. Nick told them about
Earthstar. Adam was skeptical until Nick showed him
the gyro disc. They knew it was not from Earth.

He inserted the gyro disc into the player they'd made.
Adam and Pam listened anxiously. "That explains our
vacation. It also explains the new rainbow code. But,
why didn't I know about it? I have rainbow
clearance." Adam questioned.

"You only have a limited amount of rainbow
clearance. This project is highly classified."

Nick turned off the disc player. "We've got to do
something to help them. I'm here begging you to
believe me and to keep this confidential. My friends
need help and so do we." They sat on the deck. No
one said anything. Each one knew what the other was
thinking. They wondered if Polaris would try to save
everyone. They were sure Polaris would never stop
their experiment. They wouldn't want to and most of
all, they couldn't risk the publicity. If they let the
people of Earthstar return home, everyone would learn
about the Earthstar experiment. The Earth would be
saved but Polaris would destroy Earthstar and its
inhabitants before allowing information to leak out.
The three of them felt as if the world had suddenly
ended. A lot of lives were going to be lost and only
they could prevent it. Pam and Adam were forced to
face a sticky situation. They were caught between
loyalty to Polaris Labs and their moral beliefs.

Adam and Pam drove Nick back to Polaris Town.
They decided each of them should try and come up
with a solution, no matter how impossible it seemed.
Nick hated to ruin their happiness but they were the
only adults he could trust.

 Earthstar was glowing over the horizon. It appeared
to be closer to Earth. They knew the only explanation
for the glow was radiation. Adam pulled the car over
to the side of the highway. They stared at Earthstar.
Nick wondered if the people on Earthstar could see
them. Earthstar lingered in the same position for ten
minutes, and then disappeared. Adam and Pam
dropped Nick off at home and once again they were
alone.

Adam turned off the radio. "Pam we need to talk. A
lot of lives will be lost. I wish there was something
we could do but there isn't. If we could do something,
I don't think it would be in our best interest. If we
ignore the oath we took at Polaris Labs, we may never
get work in our fields again. We have worked too hard
to get where we are. We're trying to start a new life.
I want the best for you. I can't buy the best for you on
any little salary. Think about it. We can provide our
children with their needs as well as most of the things
they want. Besides, I'm sure Polaris will do the right
thing." Pam wanted to argue but she knew Adam was
right. They shouldn't ruin their lives. Polaris Labs
weren't the enemy. Most organizations had
experimented with something. Sometimes they failed
and sometimes they succeeded. The only difference
was she knew the people involved. Polaris Labs
would not let Earthstar hit the Earth nor would they
allow all those people to die.

Something would happen and everything would be all right. Adam wasn't wrong very often. She also trusted the people at Polaris Labs. If she and Adam started making accusations and everything turned out to be okay, they would never live it down. Their lives would be ruined because they listened to a kid. Adam was right. They were going to leave this to the pros. She decided to turn her answering machine on and avoid Nicholas Andropolus Cruz II.

Mike's dog was barking erratically. "Phieffer! Be quiet!" Mike looked outside. There was nothing or anyone for him to bark at. He wondered what was wrong with his dog. "Here boy, have a biscuit." The dog continued to bark and stare at the sky. Mike's parents yelled at him. They didn't want the neighbors to get upset. Mike tried everything he could, but Phieffer would not stop barking. Mike picked up the small collie and carried him into the house. Phieffer went directly to the window. He put his front paws on the windowsill, looked up at the sky and began to bark. It was the strangest thing Mike and his parents had ever seen. Mike put on a short sleeved shirt. He had a meeting to attend. Phieffer or no Phieffer, he was now an Explorer. This was his very first meeting. The person who'd called said it was vital that he attend the meeting. It was hot outside. Sweat ran down his face. He glanced at his watch. "I've only been walking two minutes," he said. "I wonder what the temperature is. I am so hot!" Mike stopped at Polaris Mall. He bought a thirty-two ounce drink. "This should keep me from dehydrating." The Explorers' clubhouse was only ten minutes from Polaris Mall. Lenny and Max were installing a small air conditioner, when he arrived. He quickly offered to help.

Steffie Donovan leaned out the door. "How much longer?" She asked. "My blouse is starting to look like I entered a wet tee shirt competition."

"Yeah!" Lenny smiled. "And it looks like you won." She rolled her eyes and closed the door. Angie Faye handed Max two wooden planks to help support the air conditioner.

"Two by fours," Max grinned. He placed them in holes six inches deep and twelve inches apart. Later, when the cement dried, they would cover the area with dirt. The appearance of the Explorers' Clubhouse was very important to its members. The air conditioner hummed quietly. The cool air was a welcome change. Tia put Styrofoam cups and plates on the table. Steffie and Angie Faye served the refreshments.

"Where is Nick?" They asked Reggie as he entered the door.

"I thought he was already here." Reggie swallowed.

"We can't start the meeting until he gets here." Max stated. "So I guess we can relax and take advantage of the cool air and refreshments."

Nick dialed the phone again. Pam had said she and Adam would be waiting for his call. He didn't understand. Where were they? He wanted them to meet with the Explorers. Together, he was sure they would come up with a solution. The answering machine picked up on the third ring. "Please leave a message at the beep." Frustrated, Nick slammed the receiver down. A loud crash sounded at the same instant. Simultaneously, several crashes echoed throughout the house. Nick ran down the stairs. He nearly collided with Tandy, their maid. The floor was soaking wet. Fish were flopping everywhere. Somehow, all except three tanks had exploded. Nick glanced at the floor again. Nick, his mother and Tandy stood there silently. They had no idea what had caused the tanks to break. It would take a large tremor or someone beating against the glass to cause it to break like that.

Shattered glass fragments were everywhere. Tandy left the room to get mops, buckets and brooms. Nick and his mother tried to save the fish. Most of the fish were already dead. The ones, which were still alive, were convulsing. Nick picked up several fish. He noticed their heads and bodies had been crushed. He soon realized the tanks had exploded from the inside.

The three remaining tanks had less than ten fish each in them. The fish in these tanks were small tropical fish. Nick leaned closer to the tanks. The fish were floating on top of the water. The filters were slowly pulling their bodies towards them. He pressed his face closer to the glass. The heads of these fish were also crushed. He suspected mass suicide, but why? Why all the fish at the same time? Why did they break the glass? He remembered his conversation with Tia. *"Wouldn't it be great to go to the zoo, outside Polaris Town, to see if the animals are really acting freaky?"* Chills ran down his spine. He tried to control his shivering. Nick's mother suddenly remembered the Explorers' meeting. She and Tandy would call someone in to clean up the mess. Nick continued to shiver as he walked in the searing heat. The clubhouse was just across the field. He felt as if he had been walking in the heat for hours.

His legs were dragging. He felt he would pass out if he didn't get out of the heat soon. There were people running towards him. They were coming out of the ocean? Someone was calling his name but they sounded so far away. "It's getting dark," he thought. Suddenly, everything went blank.

"Can you hear me Mr. Cruz?" "Nick, open your eyes and look at me." Nick slowly opened his eyes. Everything was white. Then slowly the room and the man in front of him came into focus.
 Where was he and how did he get there? "I'm Doctor Winston," the man in white replied. "You were overcome by the heat. Lucky for you, your friends were there. They called an ambulance. You're at Polaris Medical Center. What's your name?"

"Nicholas Andropolus Cruz II," Nick answered groggily. The doctor asked him what he remembered. He remembered everything except how he'd gotten to the hospital.

"We've called your parents. They should be here soon. We will probably keep you overnight to make sure you are okay."

"Did I have a heatstroke?" Nick asked.

"Not exactly," the doctor said.

Mr. and Mrs. Cruz entered the emergency room. The nurse directed them to Nick's room. Nick motioned for Reggie to come sit beside him. He told Reggie to hold the meeting and bring everyone up to date on the situation. He also asked him to check on Pam and Adam. Nick turned on the TV. His parents left the hospital after staying only two hours. The evening news was on.

"And now for the weather report. The temperature soared beyond the old records today. It went all the way up to one hundred twelve. But that's not the worst of it. We're expecting high temperatures for the remainder of the week and into next week. So please try to stay out of the sun. If you have to be out, wear light clothing and a hat. Protect your skin. Carry a small thermos. Dehydration and heat strokes are just about inevitable in this weather. People in Enich Hills and the surrounding areas are being asked to conserve water. Don't water the lawn or wash your car. The rivers are drying up and we are in desperate need of rain. We made it through the floods. I guess we'll make it through the heat. That's it for the weather. Stay tuned for more news after this commercial break."

Nick turned off the TV. He dialed Pam's number. The phone rang constantly. "No answering machine," Nick thought. "Something is wrong. She couldn't be out of town. Someone is turning the answering machine on and off." Reggie called Nick at nine o'clock P.M. He said he'd seen Adam and Pam picking up their checks at the gates of Polaris Labs. "I'm afraid they've chickened out. They're avoiding you like the plague. But don't worry; when you get out tomorrow, we'll come up with something. Oh yeah, I almost forgot to tell you, Polaris has set up a daytime curfew. No one is allowed outside until dusk. See you tomorrow evening Nick." Nick was released the next day at six o'clock P.M.

Chapter 7—ARMAGEDDON

The entry hall and foyer were spotless. The broken
glass had been replaced but the tanks remained empty.
Nick thought how much pleasure his father had
derived from watching and breeding the fish and other
marine life. He climbed the stairs to his room,
changed clothes and crawled into bed. His mother
placed a pitcher of juice beside the bed. He drank a
glass and called Reggie. Reggie told him about
Mike's dog. Nick couldn't wait for Reggie to finish.
He had to tell him about the fish.

Pam decided to take a nap. She really wanted to see
Nick. She had heard about his accident. Polaris Town
was a small place and news traveled at the speed of
light. Adam gave her a cocktail to ease her mind. A
few minutes later she was sound asleep. Her mind
started to spin. A whirlwind began to form above her
head. It encircled her. "Wait a minute. This isn't
really a wind. It's a bunch of words. I can't read the

words. They are too small." The words grew larger.
The words: DENIAL IS THE FIRST STEP
surrounded her. The whirlwind of words lifted her off
the ground then dropped her into a burning field. The
fire was raging out of control. Voices called out from
the middle of the flames. People were running and
screaming in the midst of the fire. Familiar faces
appeared in the flames.

 She recognized her sister, the Explorers and Adam.
She wanted to reach out and help them but her fear of
the flames was horrific. Slowly, the faces melted
away. Sirens and bells could be heard in the distance.
The noise was horrible. She watched the firemen
unroll their hoses. They sprayed water on the flames
but the water seemed to be feeding the flames. The
flames licked at the firemen's jackets. Suddenly, a
fiery hand leapt from the flames and grabbed the
firemen. It dropped them in the middle of the fiery
prison with its other captives. Pam grabbed one of the
hoses. The strong smell of gasoline penetrated her
nostrils. She pulled the valve down to stop the flow of
gas. Before she could run, the fiery hand reached out
and grabbed her.

Pam sat up in her bed. Why was she having all these
nightmares? The orange numbers on the clock read
eight-thirty P.M. She told Adam about her dream. He
apologized for having the TV too loud.
He told her the sirens she heard were on the news.
"The fields near Polaris Mall burned today. No one
was hurt, but the kid's clubhouse was totaled."

"What caused the fire?" Pam asked.

"The grass is dry. Because of the temperature and the lack of rain, we'll probably have a lot more fires." The phone rang. "I forgot to tell you, your sister called."

Pam and Adam's families were coming to dinner tomorrow night. They wanted their families to get to know one another. Later they would plan the wedding. Pam wanted to get married before Christmas. She thought a winter wedding would be beautiful. Adam handed her the phone. It was good to hear her sister's voice. "Well," her sister said. "I see you've finally fallen off the deep end for a guy."

"I do like him," Pam hesitated playfully.
"Denial is the first step," her sister said. Pam dropped the phone and grabbed the end of the table to support her.

Three limos entered the gates of Polaris Town. A helicopter flew overhead. The helicopter landed on top of Polaris Labs. A second helicopter soon joined it. Everyone in Polaris Town knew what was happening. They had received calls about a very important government meeting. None of them were invited. They were simply informed to stay away from Polaris Labs. The Polaris auditorium filled quickly. There were several microphones positioned throughout the auditorium. Interpreters were seated throughout the room. The top ranking men and women of The Secret Under The Rainbow Project sat on a small stage behind the podium. Dr. Cruz approached the podium. "Our project is in trouble. We no longer have control of Earthstar. It has fallen out of its original orbit." The room became extremely noisy. Someone approached a microphone.

"Listen," he yelled in his native tongue. "We cannot learn anything or make any decisions if we don't quiet down and listen." The interpreter quickly relayed the message. The room quieted. Dr. Cruz took a deep breath. He sighed, then approached the podium, once again. He exhaled silently and began to speak.

"Earthstar has been seen in the skies around the world. All attempts to communicate with Earthstar have failed. The computers report no malfunctions but we know something is extremely wrong. The computers here at Polaris Labs are the master ground control command center for the rainbow project. Some person or persons have altered the telemetry systems. We don't know why the project has been tampered with. If the problem isn't corrected before Earthstar's next perigee, the world will look like Armageddon! We are exercising the only two options we have at the moment. One is to track the movement of Earthstar and determine its present location. This is being done at this very moment. Our observatory on Mt. Everest has the most powerful telescope in the world. The scientists there will be working nonstop to gather all possible information. The other way is to send a ship to investigate the situation. The ship will try to establish communication with Earthstar. We will be briefing the Nebula II's navigator later today The Nebula II will take photographs of Earthstar's decaying orbit. The Radiometer will measure the level of radiation around Earthstar. The Nebula II will then relay this information back to us. Once this is done, we will know if it's safe for the Nebula II to dock."

The board members raised their hands to be recognized.

"There is no time for questions. We will continue, and then try to answer as many questions as possible. Right now I'd like to introduce General Voltex of Canicula." Dr. Cruz stepped down from the podium.

A smooth bronze skinned man with white hair approached the podium. "I'm afraid what I have to say is worse than what you have already heard. Your saboteur probably thought he knew all about the rainbow project. However, he did not know that scientists from both planets designed a program to keep the project a secret. If Earthstar comes to close to Earth or any of its equipment is damaged; an electromagnetic transmitter sends a signal to the master core of the main reactor. The result is an immediate meltdown."
"What reactor?" A voice yelled.

"Please, bear with me. Everything will be explained. A small nuclear charge was installed in each computer system." The general wiped the sweat from his brow. "Each of your towns has at least one of these systems. All of the reactors are controlled by the main computer telemetry and temperature regulator functions. When your core melts the chain reaction will be like the domino effect. There will be no traces of evidence that this project or anything else ever existed. A lot of lives in nearby towns will be lost. But, they are expendable. I realize you feel cheated. We thought it would be better for everyone involved if we kept this information a secret as long as possible. We have got to get all the information we need immediately or we won't have time to reprogram the computer without detonating the reactors. In closing ladies and gentlemen, I suggest you either find a way to get that damned planetoid back in orbit or get the hell out of Dodge!"

"Dr. Cruz, I believe you can handle it from here." The general stated as he left the building. The members were horrified. Their minds conjured up scenes of World War II and the aftermath of the Atomic Bomb. The Nazi experiments on the Jews; slavery and mass executions seemed civilized compared to what might happen to billions of people. Innocent people would be sacrificed for the advancement of scientific knowledge and the making of a superior race. They thought about horrible punishments for the villain. Then they realized they too shared the blame with the culprit.

Was any one person really responsible for this mess? Weren't they all equally responsible? If only they could regain control in time. Dr. Cruz began to speak.

"The general said we would have a delayed reaction time. This will occur after the final signal from Earthstar is received from ground control. This will give us the time we need to evacuate our cities and the surrounding areas. Let's hope we don't need it."

Professor Donovan stood up. "What you have learned today is a great shock to all of you. It's time to make a decision. The color-coded sectors have kept the other members of Polaris Town and the other I.S.S.A towns in the dark. We may have to awaken them to the possibility of living their worst nightmares."

"According to our scientist on Mt. Everest, we have approximately one hundred twenty hours to come up with a solution. Everyone will report back to his or her prospective cities immediately after the meeting. Transportation has been arranged. You may submit all suggestions to Dr. Samantha Quartz. If there is no further business to discuss, we will begin the question and answer period. This meeting will adjourn immediately afterwards."

The meeting ended with a majority vote to keep the other employees and the public in the dark.

A lone figure entered Polaris Guest Hotel. The elevator took him to penthouse one. He was weary and disgusted. The meeting had frightened everyone but it simply made him angry. They were trying to make him confess. Their claims that people would die and the world would end were blasphemous. He crawled into bed. He needed sleep. If he rested his mind, he would know what to do. The room was cool. He slowly drifted to sleep. Dreams rushed into his head. The sky glowed red. It was extremely hot; people were running through the streets. The heat was stifling. People fainted and fell on the hot pavement. A tall stranger watched as others treaded over and on them. The heat made it difficult to breathe. He could see people ripping off their clothing trying to get cool. Two teenagers ran past the stranger screaming. The heat had burned their skin raw. Putrid skin was peeling off their bodies in large bloody chunks.

One of the teens opened his mouth to say something. Steam poured from his mouth and nostrils. He looked towards the stranger pleading for his life. Twenty seconds later, he exploded. Blood and meat flew in all directions but no one seemed to notice. They had their own plights to deal with. The stranger looked up. He saw two little naked children flying towards him. "You could have prevented this," they said. "If you'd only believed. Your thoughts were not wrong. The problem was you did not take the time to think about the consequences of your actions. You must right the wrongs. You must tell the people, all the people. They have a right to know. Look." The little cherubs pointed towards the sky. "Even now, the destruction is upon them."

The stranger looked up. The sun was falling. A young girl reached up to him. The skin was dripping from her hands. The stranger tried to tell her to get out of the heat, but it was too late. Her face began to melt. Her eyeballs slid down the soggy place that was once her face. The man sat up in bed and screamed.

Pam decided to go to Polaris Mall. She needed a new tablecloth and also wanted to buy some last minute items for the dinner. She prayed her family would like Adam's family. The sales person showed her a peach linen tablecloth, white lace runners and matching accessories. The table was going to be beautiful. She purchased a new dress and shoes after leaving the linen shop. Everything had to look perfect, including her. Stopping in front of the Wedding Boutique, she saw a beautiful peach wedding gown displayed in the window. Backing away from the window, she bumped into someone passing by.

"Excuse me," she said turning around to face the person.

"You're excused," Nick grunted. Pam felt she'd shrunk five feet. Nick didn't give her the opportunity to talk.

"You didn't have to avoid me. You could have just said you changed your mind."

"Nick," she explained. "You don't understand. Polaris would never let all those bad things happen. They are going to fix everything. You'll see everything will be back to normal very soon. That's why they had that big meeting today."

"Sure Pam," Nick smirked. "I'll bet your wedding dress is gonna look real good covered in the blood of your friends." Nick turned and walked away. "Adam was right. Nick is a spoiled brat. I'm not going to let him ruin tonight." Pam quickly finished her shopping. She wanted to get away from Polaris Town and Nick. "I don't understand Nick. He has never acted like this before. We have always been the best of friends." She tried to convince herself that everything would be okay once Polaris solved this problem.

The dinner party was a success. It was hard to believe the two families had never met. The women laughed and talked while clearing the dinner table. The men watched the news and discussed things that only men could enjoy talking about. Adam raised the volume on the TV.

"Well, the newsman laughed, *it didn't rain over Moscow. However, four communications satellites fell near the city this morning. The area has been listed as a restricted zone. To quote the Russian news*

*reporter; "Thank God, the satellites fell in an
unpopulated area outside the city." In other world
news, two planes crashed in London. No one
survived. The black boxes have been located. The
plane that crashed over Mexico, last Thursday, was
ruled an accident."*

*" According to the pilot, some type of electromagnetic
field disrupted the plane's guidance system. The
investigation showed the guidance system had been
altered. The strange thing about this is the watches of
all the passengers alive and dead stopped exactly one
hour before the crash. Well, I'm Dick Johnson and
that's it for the ten o'clock news".*

Pam and Adam cuddled on the sofa. They enjoyed
their guests, now once again they were alone. Pam
climbed into bed at twelve thirty. The nightly news
had depressed her. Seven strange airplane crashes,
two helicopter crashes and no sign of the torrid
temperatures easing up. Perhaps, the news would be
better tomorrow.

Pam found herself the victim of another horrible
nightmare. The Earth was hot and barren. It
appeared all the inhabitants of Earth were dead. She
alone had survived. Bodies were strewn everywhere.
The heat and stench of the rotting flesh were
intolerable. A long narrow road glowed from the
radioactive dust. She decided to follow the road.
She hoped it would lead to a city, which was still
standing, or to other survivors. The life she had
known was over. Pam had no intention of being the
last woman on Earth. If the radiation didn't kill her,
then she would have to do the job herself.

The road seemed to go on forever. A movement on the road ahead caught her attention. A young boy sat crouched on the side of the road. He slowly lifted his hairless head. His blank colorless eyes stared aimlessly ahead. Pam felt relieved. The little boy was dehydrated but he was alive. The little boy had something in his hand. She pried the plastic rainbow card from his frail hand. Adam's face stared at her from the card. Pam questioned the boy. "Where did you find this? Where is the owner of it?"

The boy said nothing. She had to know where Adam was. She shook the boy profusely.

"Where did you get this?"

The boy slowly raised his right arm. He pointed to a man twenty feet away. The man was lying face down. He was wearing a silk blue robe and shorts. The man had been dead for days. She rolled him over and screamed. He had no face. On the road behind her, the little boy's eyes rolled back in his head. He opened his toothless mouth and cried, "Help me Pam!"

Pam opened her eyes. The daylight was a welcome sight. Why was she having such atrocious nightmares? She had to get her head together. Adam snored quietly. She envied him. Climbing out of bed, she headed for the kitchen.

The coffee brewed slowly. Glancing at the clock, she realized it was only six fifteen. The morning news would be depressing but she needed the company. A newsperson walked in front of the camera.

"We're sorry for the inconvenience this morning. Some nut, who thinks he's the Pope, has been trying to get a moment of airtime.

We have tried to put him out several times. He claims to have a life and death message. Since we're an early morning show and we generally try to provide entertainment, we're going to let the nut talk. So here he is, the man who claims to be Pope Solomon Micah". The studio quieted. Someone pulled the newscaster aside.

"You stupid bitch! That is Pope Solomon Micah!" She immediately ran to microphone and apologized. She reintroduced the Pope.

"And now, His Holiness, Pope Solomon Micah." The newscaster's face was red with embarrassment.

Pope Solomon Micah sat at a blue and yellow newscaster's desk.

"I am not trying to panic you.   But, I feel that you deserve to know the truth. The I.S.S.A wanted to keep this a secret.   First, I ask you and the churches to forgive me for sinning.   However, I can never forgive myself. After I have finished talking to you, I'll be leaving for the Vatican."

"I will beg to be forgiven and allowed to present my resignation.   Please tell everyone what you hear from me today.   It is vital for everyone to know the truth. I also want you to understand the I.S.S.A is trying to solve the problem.   I pray they will."

"I have wronged the people, my faith and most of all myself. I have failed to be a spiritual leader. I have allowed and participated in an experiment instituted by the I.S.S.A. They set up towns all around the world. The best scientists, technicians, engineers and their families occupy these towns. The closet town to Enich Hills, Tennessee is Polaris Town. People of the world, think! Were there any towns built outside of your town within the last ten years?"

"Towns, where the children don't attend your schools. The people don't shop at your stores or work with you or your neighbors. These are the I.S.S.A towns. They were designed for one purpose. To create a planetoid similar to Earth but more advanced. This planetoid now exists. The space flights you've financed and cheered weren't just for exploration. They were taking the planetoid up, piece by piece. This planetoid is called Earthstar."
"The people who populate Earthstar will never be missed because you don't know them. They are all a part of an experiment called The Secret Under The Rainbow. Parents volunteer to abduct their own children and become part of this new world. This may not sound bad to you. You may even think you'd like to participate. But this is only the beginning of the story."

Reggie called members of the Explorers Club and told them to get up and watch the news. Pam rushed into the bedroom. She turned the TV on and awoke Adam.

"This planet is composed of one third humans and one third alien life forms. These aliens are called Caniculiens. They are from the planet Canicula.

They look identical to us, with the exception of their octagon shaped eyes. Their skin is light brown or bronze."

"The purpose of Earthstar is to breed humans and Caniculiens together to make a race of stronger super intelligent beings. Leviticus nineteenth chapter, twenty-third verse states: Neither shall any woman stand before a beast to lie down there to, it is confusion. Leviticus nineteenth chapter, twenty-sixth verse states: You shall therefore keep my statues and my judgment, and shall not commit any of these abominations; neither any of your own nation, nor any stranger that sojourns among you."

"These heathen aliens will corrupt our children morally and spiritually. These poor souls are being held captive on Earthstar. Both the Caniculien children and our children want to go home. Earthstar is like a prison state. Armed guards constantly watch the people. The I.S.S.A and Canicula have absolute authority. This type of authority corrupts people when used without conscience or responsibility."

"This new race they are trying so hard to breed will have no ties to humanity. God created the heavens, Earth and man. Man will create the new inhabitants of Earthstar. Their moral obligations will be almost nonexistent."

"I made the mistake of playing God. I thought if I tampered with the master computers, it would cause the experiment to be aborted. I wanted to scare the I.S.S.A and make them think about what they were doing. I should have told the truth about this project a long time ago.   Earthstar is now in danger and so are you.   Earthstar has fallen out of orbit and is heading towards the Earth's atmosphere.   The thing you have been seeing in the skies around the world is Earthstar. The disasters happening around the globe are because of Earthstar tilting towards Earth.   Look for more and more natural disasters and more torrid conditions."

The scientists had been ordered to track Earthstar's orbit. They pushed the buttons to open the sliding doors that housed the giant telescope.   One scientist gently pressed the red button to extend and position the telescope.   It was positioned seventy miles ahead of Earthstar's last position.   Earthstar was spotted immediately.   What the scientist saw was a large shining sphere.   It illuminated the sky with such brilliance that no moons or stars could be seen in their field of vision. The scientist temporarily blinded stumbled away from the telescope.   Once the effect of the light had worn off, they decided to photograph Earthstar on special plates. The photographs of Earthstar showed a multi-colored surface. They knew this was due to excessive heat from radiation and absorption of too much energy.   There were places where internal ruptures had occurred. A breech of Synacom 14 was inevitable. Shielding materials made of Synacom 14 would be necessary for repairs and timing would be critical.

Admiral Bradford had been briefed on his mission. This mission was vitally important to the I.S.S.A but it was equally as important to him.   His family was on Earthstar and he wanted them back. He ignited the engine and prepared for lift off.   This time he didn't have time to enjoy the scenery.   He was instructed to proceed at the highest velocity possible. The Nebula II zoomed into Earthstar's orbit.

Admiral Bradford was horrified at the appearance of Earthstar. He felt sad and disgusted. "Get it together," he told himself. "This isn't going to help your family." He quickly gained his composure and turned his attention to the task at hand. The camera taking pictures of Earthstar had to be altered constantly because of Earthstar's unstable orbit. The pictures were shocking.

The I.S.S.A had thought of Earthstar as the Titanic of space, a vessel invincible to the perils of space. Admiral Bradford relayed a message back to Polaris. He explained why docking would be impossible.

"Earthstar does not have the velocity needed to stabilize its orbit. The only reason it is still in orbit is because of the gravitational pull of the moon. If it drops out of orbit with the moon it's Earth bound. I'm detecting extremely high levels of radiation up here. The closer I get to Earthstar, the higher the radiation levels rise. The environmental control beacons are still operational. I'm positive everyone is still alive."

Admiral Bradford was told to relay all information and photographs to the backup computers then return home. As the Nebula II prepared to return home, the moon jerked and Earthstar tilted towards Earth. She slowly began her descent towards the Earth.

Toby awoke slowly. He rubbed his eyes and stared at the light fixtures. The lights seemed to be slanted. He decided to hop out of bed and wash his face. He jumped up instead of down. "What the hell is going on?" He reached for the phone and quickly dialed The Brain. The Brain told him to attach weights to his ankles to help fight the effects of gravity. Toby hung up the phone. The ankle weights he'd received in gym class were in the top drawer of his desk. He quickly buckled the five-pound weights to his ankles. This gave him a little more leverage. He was still hovering three feet above the floor. His mother entered the room.

"Why aren't you floating?" He asked.
"The gravitational pull must not be as strong on adults. Are you feeling sick?" After realizing Toby was fine, she told him everyone was quarantined to his or her homes.

People were reporting to the hospital with symptoms of radiation sickness. Toby looked at the crystals he'd found. They were glowing fiercely. The temperature in the house was rising. Toby's Mom set the thermostat to its lowest setting. A black van pulled into their driveway. Toby's father opened the door.

A pudgy man dressed in a reflective suit, which covered his entire body, got out of the van.

"I'm from the research labs. My name is Dr. Sorflet. Please call your family."

Toby's father escorted the man into the den. Toby and his Mom had been listening from the hall. The man removed three metallic badges from his pocket. He grabbed Toby's finger and drew a small amount of blood from it. The blood was placed in a small tube. He then, removed a metallic badge from its case and pinned it on Toby's shirt. His mother was next and then his father. One by one the man put a drop of their blood on their badges.

The badges absorbed the blood. Toby and his mother looked at their badges. Their badges glowed yellow. They were frightened. Twenty seconds later, the badges were back to normal. The man wrote something in a small book.

"Are we contaminated?" His mother gasped.

"No," the man replied. "That was a normal reaction."

 Toby's father's badge glowed yellow and then a sickly green color.

"I'm sorry," the man told him. "But you'll have to come with us." He was ushered into the back of the van. Dr. Sorflet told Toby and his mother to wear the badges at all times. "If they turn green call the number on the back." The van drove to Brain's house.

Toby and his mother huddled together on the couch. They were trying to console each other.   Save yourselves and forgive me for what I've done to you; were the last words Toby would ever hear from his father. Toby looked out the window. No one was taken from The Brain's house. He had to talk to The Brain. They had to help his father. He wondered if his father was still alive.
 Toby's mother handed him a strange looking pill.

"This should help our bodies fight off radiation." Loud creaking noises seemed to be coming from all around them. It sounded like Earthstar was falling apart. The house shook violently. Toby and his mother were afraid. He ran downstairs and called The Brain.

The Brain instructed them to gather supplies and go into the basement shelter. Toby hurried off the phone. His mother was sitting on the couch. He explained what they had to do. She told Toby it was too late for her. She removed her hands from her chest. Her badge was glowing green.

"I'm not leaving you Mom." He screamed. She'd packed can goods and other supplies in a suitcase.

"I called Mrs. Bradford," she said. "I know they will take good care of you. Toby, I want you to always remember your father and I love you. We never intended to cause you any harm. Remember Toby, we love you." She pushed Toby out of the house.

The sharp razor cut deeply into her wrists. There was hardly any pain. Toby watched through the window as his mother bled to death. The Brain's mother explained to him what was happening at Toby's house. The Brain looked outside. Toby was sitting on the porch with his face against the window. Brain walked across the lawn to Toby's house. Looking through the window, he saw Toby's mother lying on the floor in a puddle of blood. He pulled Toby to his feet and grabbed the suitcase. The Brain led Toby to his house. A tremor knocked them off their feet. It felt like a point six on the Richter scale.

The Brain crawled across the lawn dragging both the suitcase and Toby. Mrs. Bradford met them at the door. She told Brain to take Toby into the basement. After helping Toby, he continued to stock the basement. The TV and radio were the last items on the list. Looking out the window, Mrs. Bradford realized they were going to be underground for a long time.

"Dad will be here, right Mom?" The Brain asked. An eerie orange and gray mist hovered over the neighborhood. The Brain took one last look then went below.

Chapter 8—DECEPTION

A loud beeping sound came from the portable TV on the table near the control panel at Mt. Everest observatory.

"We interrupt this program for a special news report. A major earthquake hit along the San Andreas Fault. The quake was felt from Mexico to Washington. Thousands of miles of shore have fallen into the Pacific Ocean. Countless lives have been destroyed. The death toll is just above three thousand and rising. This is the worst disaster in the history of the United States. The earthquake measured ten on the Richter scale. Survivors are bracing themselves for the aftershocks. We have reporters on the scene now. Tom, are you there?"

"Yeah, Bill. It's horrible. Bodies are everywhere. Can you see the fires behind me? There's nothing left. It's like a whole slab of California was just sliced off

*and now there's nothing! There are people down
there. People buried alive. God, it's horrible!"*

*"We're going to give you time to get yourself together.
Tom. We now return to your regular program. We
will keep you abreast of the situation. "*

Hans, the youngest astronomer looked over the
information sent by the Nebula II. He noticed a large
circle of light reflecting from Earthstar. "I wonder if
the light contains enough radiation to harm Earth. I
know Synacom 14 is not generally affected by heat or
radiation, but?" He thought.
"Does Synacom 14 have the ability to deflect heat
and radiation?"

He asked Dr. Cruz to fax him a file on Synacom 14.
The astronomers shouted joyously when they read the
test results of the metallurgists and chemists.
Synacom 14's density and durability far exceeded
their expectations. Their joy ended when they
compared the radiation levels to blueprints and
schematics of Earthstar. They never imagined the
maximum stress levels could be exceeded. The
astronomers told Polaris Labs to instruct the Nebula
II to return to Earthstar and take a spectral reading and
transmit it to them immediately. The Nebula II's
report confirmed the maximum stress levels had been
exceeded. It also showed Earthstar's internal
structure had weakened. As the Nebula II prepared to
return home the lights on the central panel began to
blink.

"What now?" Admiral Bradford wondered.
Everything checked out fine. There were no
malfunctions. "The lights aren't just blinking. They

are flashing in sequence. It's Morse code! Earthstar is trying to communicate with me."

He sent a message immediately. A few seconds later, he received a message from Professor Norvin.

We need to evacuate immediately. People are beginning to show signs of radiation sickness. The gravity is unstable. Most of the people have gone underground. We are rounding up the people with radiation sickness.

Most of them are too far gone to help. Earthstar is unstable. But there is a way for ships to dock. You'll have to dock when Earthstar is facing the light side of the moon. If our calculations are correct, you should have no problem. We only have two operational docking areas. Please let us know when you are ready. I realize it will take six ships to remove all of Earthstar's inhabitants. There won't be enough time to do this, even if the ships were already in position. There will be a great loss of life. I will try to decide the best way to handle this situation. I'll expect to hear from you within the next ten hours.

The news of the Pope's announcement spread quickly. The I.S.S.A called an emergency meeting. The meeting would be held in Polaris Town. The purpose of the meeting was to discuss what steps should be taken to avoid publicity and discovery of The Secret Under The Rainbow. The meeting was scheduled at twenty three hundred hours.

The auditorium had standing room only. It took thirty minutes for everyone to be seated and twenty extra minutes to get them quiet. Dr. Cruz addressed the crowd.

"Ladies and gentlemen, I suppose you have all heard about the implications made by His Holiness, Pope Solomon Micah. We are here to come up with a workable solution. We need to dispute all allegations directed towards the I.S.S.A. We have got to avoid discovery. I now yield the floor to you for any suggestions."

Several individuals expressed their opinions. "The obvious thing to do would be to admit the truth and take our punishments. However, if we do this we would tarnish the reputation of some of the greatest minds this world will ever know."

"Why not haul the Pope back to Polaris Town? We could force him to give us the access codes."

"Why not kill him and make it look like an accident?" Some of the suggestions were getting outrageous. Dr. Cruz decided to take control.

"We know the press is going to investigate the Pope's implications. We have no intention of letting one piece of evidence be found. At this time, the chair recognizes General Andrew DeWitt."

General DeWitt stood in front of the crowd. "We need to stop the leak at its source. The television audience's first impression of Pope Solomon Micah was that of a raving lunatic trying to get the media's attention. Every tabloid in the world has probably covered a UFO story at some point. People love to believe in little green men. If we linked his implications to a delusion, nobody would believe him. I caution you to be careful. Don't incriminate yourselves by making the signs of his mental lapse look staged. We must discredit him so others will think him mad."

Adam tossed the suitcase in the trunk of the car. A security box was hidden beneath the spare. He had convinced Pam to close their bank accounts and leave town until the crisis ended. The food and drinks were on the floorboard of the back seat. The only thing missing was the satellite TV and emergency supplies. The morning news proved Nick was right. Pam wanted to apologize but it was too late. Adam told her everyone was being transferred out of Polaris Town. He said all I.S.S.A towns were being altered to look like research facilities. The remaining people and their families would move into hotels in the towns. It would appear to outsiders the families were visiting the workers.

Pam's faith in the I.S.S.A had been badly shaken. She wasn't sure what to believe. This trip would do her a lot of good. She and Adam were meeting their families on the Gulf Coast. They were going to marry immediately. This wasn't exactly the way she'd planned on getting married. However, she needed to escape the chaos of Polaris and her association with it.

Pam watched the news as they drove down the highway. The story given by the Pope was repeated. More natural disasters were reported and fires raged around the world. The final report was on satellites falling from space. Phone companies were asking people to limit calls. The television went fuzzy and the station was gone.

"Did you see that?" Pam gasped. Adam turned the radio on. All he got was static. He tried several stations. Finally he found an audible station. They passed more than a dozen stalled cars. The heat was taking its toll on everything. The weatherman had said the temperature would reach between one hundred ten and one hundred fifteen degrees. Emergency shelters were overrun with people trying to keep cool.

Pam glanced at a billboard. The advertisement for a restaurant ten miles ahead read: The best food and the coolest air conditioners in the south. Pam and Adam decided to stop and have dinner.
It was the thought of dining in an extremely cool place that attracted them. The restaurant was crowded. The food and air were great. They also had large screen TVs around the walls for sporting events. No one was watching sports. They were waiting for the news. Adam and Pam were seated in the rear of the restaurant. The atmosphere was casual and small townish.

"This is a special report from the Vatican City with Wayne Lowe." A light skinned black man stood outside the gates of the Vatican.

"Pictures of aliens with bulging eyes and large craniums were found in the Pope's living quarters. Also found were collages of alien drawings with human heads and body parts. Here are some of the pictures we took while inside the Pope's room."

The film showed close-ups of UFOs, videotapes of old science fiction movies and rubber masks and gloves with suction cups on them. Erector sets, plastic creatures and toy robots lined the shelves. The cameras were once again on Wayne Lowe. Slowly he turned around, disguised in one of the latex alien masks and gloves.

"Rational or irrational?" He laughed and removed the costume. *"One of the most revealing items found was the Pope's personal diary of dreams. What's so weird about that? Under each entry he tried to pacify himself with a rational explanation of each nightmare. They say you can always find out about a person by visiting his home. Well, proof or no proof, this kind of makes you wonder, doesn't it? The Catholic Church had no comments. We will be back in six hours with another special report. His Holiness, Pope Solomon Micah will give us a tour of one of the I.S.S.A towns. This is Wayne Lowe returning you to your regular program."*
Adam and Pam finished their meals. They planned to drive another forty or fifty miles then check into a hotel. The waitress told them a bad storm was headed their way. They didn't want to be driving when it started. The sky was sunny and it was extremely hot. Pam couldn't imagine it storming. "Maybe the storm will make the temperature drop."

The I.S.S.A towns were chaotic. Bulldozers, cranes and other machines worked all night to level the houses and malls. Families were taken to private airports and flown to secret locations.
The materials from the leveled buildings were loaded in trucks and hauled away. The sun glowed brightly on the new I.S.S.A towns. The grounds were covered

in concrete. Several metal warehouses stood in places where houses and parks had been. Storage areas where malls had stood surrounded small restaurants. In Polaris Town, a large weather balloon was placed in an empty airplane hangar. It was an exact replica of Earth. The I.S.S.A was just about ready to meet the press. Sod, flowers and trees were planted around the storage areas. Dust was spread inside the storage areas to make them appear old and unused.

Only five of the original Explorers were still in Polaris Town. The only new members left were Mike and Steffie. Nick missed his friends. He felt like another puppet on the I.S.S.A's strings. His mother told him, things had changed for their protection. Like it or not they were an I.S.S.A family. Mrs. Cruz knew it was time to put her foot down. She forbade him to interfere. He would not be allowed to leave his room without his parents until the reporters left. Nick felt his punishment was unfair.

Cars lined up for miles outside the gates of Polaris Town. The I.S.S.A promised to open the gates of all their towns for inspection. The gates were to be opened at three o'clock. People began lining up at twelve. The first eighty cars to enter the gates were reporters and cameramen. The Pope and two of his bodyguards were in the eighty-first car.

People from surrounding towns poured in by the hundreds. Hundreds of folding chairs were arranged in a parking lot. Dr. Cruz watched impatiently from the doorway of Polaris Labs. He was angry with the people and the Pope. He saw mothers with picnic baskets and blankets. Children were screaming and playing. They were making a circus out of Polaris

Town. He hated dealing with such ignorance. "I know this has to be done. I've got to save the reputation of the I.S.S.A and its employees."

The Pope, news reporters and other special guests were escorted to the front row seats. People were taking pictures of everything including the parking lot. Dr. Donovan introduced himself to the crowd. He explained the purpose of the I.S.S.A towns. Several buses were waiting in a nearby parking lot.

"You can't all fit in the same area at the same time. Each tour will start in a different area. I assure you, you will see the same things. There are some top secret areas you are not allowed in, but that's to be expected. It would be the same way if you visited a brewery."

"Now if our special guests would join Dr. Quartz here." He said pointing to a woman in a white lab coat. "They will be escorted to the first tour bus. The rest of you, please gather with your friends and families and you will be assigned a bus."

Pope Solomon Micah glanced around while walking towards the bus. He was amazed. It was like the town was totally rebuilt. The tour began with a drive along Polaris' fenced boundaries. Dr. Quartz explained what the different storage buildings were used for. The buildings were dusty and stale. Some of them smelled as if they hadn't been opened in years.   There was a small airport near the south boundary. Two private planes and one helicopter sat quietly on the runways. They entered a large hangar. A huge replica of Earth was inside. Dr. Quartz told the people about the tests Polaris Labs had been conducting with it.

The Pope was so awe struck; he could say nothing in his defense. He simply shook his head. The next stop was Polaris Guest Hotel. They were introduced to a few families who were visiting their relatives. The children appeared to be normal children. They wore name brand clothing, had weird hairstyles and used slang just like other kids.

One reporter said, "These kids are no smarter than my own kids." The children told the reporters they enjoyed visiting their families, but there was nothing to do here so they were bored and ready to go home. One boy complained about not being able to play ball. A young girl said, "I like watching TV. My Mom and I will be leaving in two days. I will miss my grandfather but I want to be where I can have fun."

The people were told the families were allowed to visit for two weeks every six months. The next stop on the tour was Polaris Labs. They watched some of the experiments being conducted. The last stop was the command center and the Nebulas' launch pad. Refreshments were placed on several long tables in the parking lot. A large canopy and fans helped to cool the crowds. The air was warm but it felt good.

Dr. Cruz approached the podium. "I hope all of you enjoyed your tours and found them interesting. I'm sure no one found any alien monsters lurking about." The crowd looked at the Pope and then burst into a fit of laughter. The Pope ran to the microphones. He was waving his hands trying to quiet the crowds. The people finally quieted down.

"I'll expose them all!" He yelled. "I can name names. I know all of the top people involved. They are trying to frame me. They are trying to make me look like a raving lunatic!"

"You're doing a pretty good job of that yourself!" Someone yelled.

"I have proof! If you'd just listen to me! I am the Pope! I don't lie. I could never lie!"

A man from the I.S.S.A approached the Pope. "If you agree to submit to a psychiatric evaluation," he said into the microphone. "And allow us to release the findings as well as information about your life prior to becoming Pope." The Pope knew he was being set up. "Then," the man said. "We will allow you to tell the world what you have to say. That is, if you're sane."
The man and the audience waited for the Pope to respond. The Pope was trapped. He had no alternative but to agree to the tests. He knew his fate was now in the hands of God. He smiled to himself because he knew his fate did not rest in the hands of the I.S.S.A. He quietly agreed to the tests.

"That's it for our tour," Dr. Cruz smiled. He knew they had succeeded. "Please return to your vehicles. Polaris' gates will close in two hours."

Chapter 9—A REVELATION!

Nick stared at the television. He heard the tour
groups when they passed his door. Every station with
power carried Polaris' shenanigan. Tia and the other
Explorers played their parts well.

"Cute innocent little children visiting their families.
What a hoax," he groaned. When the television
broadcast ended, Nick realized what the I.S.S.A was
up too. "They intend to have Pope Solomon Micah
committed. I've got to talk to the Pope." Nick picked
up the phone. He dialed Reggie's room. Reggie was
also confined to his room. He was considered as
much of a threat to the project as Nick was.

Reggie suggested using Mike and Tia to do their spying. "No one knows they are members of The Explorers Club. Mike is so innocent looking; all the adults think he is the sweetest little kid. I'll call you later. I've got to contemplate our next move." Reggie knew Mike was only eleven years old, but he was just as sneaky as he was cute.

The Pope was flown to an undisclosed building outside Washington. There he would submit to a battery of psychiatric tests. He was escorted to a small room. The room had an extremely long single bed, a nightstand and a small dresser. A reading lamp was connected to the headboard. The sunlight seemed to reflect off the bleached white walls.

A small closet with white pants and shirts seemed to enhance the look of purity. Two pairs of white shoes were neatly arranged on the floor of the closet. One pair was slippers and the other loafers. The drawers contained white underwear, nightshirts and socks. The nightstand drawer had a small white Bible and personal items.

Pope Solomon Micah glanced disgustedly around the room.

"Where's the phone?"

"Phones aren't allowed in the patient's rooms. But if you're a good little nut, we'll let you use the office phone once in a while." The orderly laughed and locked the door behind him. There was another door behind the Pope. He opened the door hoping to find an exit.

"I should have known. It's just a bathroom." He stared into the mirror. A sad solemn figure stared back at him. He kneeled down and began to pray.

Dr. Lambert stared at the manila file on his desk. It was getting late and he was ready to go home. This was a top priority file.

"It's been a long day. I really don't care if they lock this guy up for life or not. I'll glance at the file, prescribe some tests, administer drug-laced food before the test and make a quick decision. Mr. Breshner thinks aliens are attacking the world. His delusions are becoming dangerous and he's a threat to the nursing home he lives in."

Dr. Lambert tossed the file aside. "He's definitely a nut." He felt guilty about being too judgmental without giving the man a chance. "Well, maybe he's not." He began to read the file again. "Mr. Breshner was an electronics engineer and a computer analytical genius. His chief job was to design programs for aerodynamic flight and build simulators for the space program."
"He was a member of a subversive club known as The UFO Seekers. He couldn't meet the requirements for actual flight, so he designed programs to make him feel as though he was really flying. Oh yeah! He is a nut! Look at all the junk he keeps in his room."

The Pope had just finished his dinner. It was not the best food, but at least it was palatable.

"Mr. Breshner, I'm Dr. Lambert." A short balding man in his late fifties stood in the doorway. "I'm glad to see the clothes fit. My staff does quite well in that department. Come with me please."

The Pope walked behind the doctor. Two orderlies followed closely behind. The long white halls seemed to go on forever. Someone was screaming. He glanced in the direction of the scream.

"How many innocent people have been confined in this place, sentenced to a life of doom and false accusations," he wondered. The long hall swayed to the left. They passed a sign that read: Adolescence. A child was praying.

"Please let Mommy come back and get me. They hurt me here. Please Lord, come and get me out of here. I'll be good. I won't hurt little Billy anymore. I promise. I'll be good."

The Pope mumbled a silent prayer for the child and all other children like her. He glanced up. The hall started to slant and the lights were glowing brightly. How did they expect him to walk down a slanted hall? They stopped in front of a set of slanted doors. The walls in the room were glowing. A white table and three chairs were the only furnishing. The room began to bend into undulating lines. It was like watching the entire scene through gas fumes. He stumbled towards the table. His body weighed a ton. Someone was watching him. They thought he didn't see them, but they couldn't hide from him. He knew their skin color blended in with the walls. One of them moved. He wasn't going to let them get him. They wanted him dead. They knew he would tell and the people would believe him.

The orderlies stood against the wall. Dr. Lambert questioned his patient thoroughly. He asked him hypothetical and literal questions. The Pope answered the questions to the best of his distorted ability. His answers were truthful and quick. During his evaluation, he continued to glance at the wall. Dr. Lambert wrote notes on his pad; needs extensive psychoanalytic psychotherapy. He and the orderlies left the room. They entered the observation room. The doctor sat at a desk near a large two-way mirror. He turned on the intercom.

"Be seated, Mr. Breshner. I am going to project a few pictures on the wall. I want you to relax. I will be recording your reactions to the pictures. Soft music will be piped into the room. Once the slides are finished, I will turn the lights on and the evaluation will be over."

The lights dimmed slowly until the Pope was in complete darkness. A picture of a red rose appeared on the wall. The rose was huge and growing larger. He rubbed his eyes and the picture changed. A large black crow was staring at him. Soft music began to play; wordless music, music that contained the cry of an evil crow. The crow stretched out his large wings. He emitted a high pitched scream then flew directly towards the Pope. The bird was going to kill him. The Pope grabbed his head and ducked under the table. He glanced around the room. The crow had vanished. The room was dark again, except for the light coming from the projector. He crawled from under the table. Why had they left him alone?

"Oh my God, they're coming for me!" Small white aliens with glowing bodies wrenched themselves from the walls. "Help, Help me!" Dr. Lambert reached for his microphone.

"I'm sorry Mr. Breshner, but the projector is not acting right."

The Pope looked up. He was surrounded. The small aliens launched forward. The Pope screamed. "Get the jacket," Dr. Lambert yelled. The orderlies went form code green to code yellow. They ran into the room with the Pope. They quickly wrestled him to the ground and sedated him. The Strait jacket was laced and the Pope was taken back to his room where he was strapped to the bed
.

Darkness was all around him. Shaken and drowsy, he bowed his head and began to pray. "How can I pass on the knowledge, so the world can know the truth? It does not matter whether I live or die. If it is your will that I be thought of as a mad man, then let it be. I only wish the truth to be known."

He closed his eyes and drifted off to sleep. He dreamed of death and destruction. There were blood curdling screams and chaos all around. A voice called from amidst the smoke and flames.

"Solomon! Solomon Micah! Open your eyes and look upon me." He opened his eyes. The light in the room was so bright; he had to shield his eyes.

"Uncover your eyes." A light female voice drifted through the room like a sweet musical note. "Open your eyes and see what will become of those you leave behind."

"I can't. The light is too bright." The Pope rubbed his eyes.

"Your eyes will adjust to the light. The light you see is the light of hope."

He opened his eyes. A golden skinned child dressed in a white silken gown and a halo stood before him. Her hair was long and coppery. She appeared to be nine or ten years old. But, she spoke with the wisdom of time. Her bronze feet were bare. She hovered four feet above the floor. Something moved near her shoulders. Wings, she had beautiful white feathery wings.
"An angel; I'm either dreaming, hallucinating or the Lord is sending her to answer my prayers."

"Believe what you see." The angel replied. "If your prayers for the world are to be answered, you must find the courage you'll need to endure the hardships that will be inflicted upon you."

"I will do whatever the Lord wills of me." The Pope responded. "I wish to receive absolution for my sins. Will the Lord grant me this?" He asked.

"He has already forgiven you. But, there's a child called Nick. He has lost faith in his parents and those whom he put his trust in. You must speak to him. Help him to regain his love and trust in humanity. This child has a special purpose in life." The angel bowed her head. "If he turns bad, all hope will be lost. It is only through remembrance of one's mistakes that learning and wisdom is obtained."

The Pope looked puzzled. "I am locked in here. How can I get to this child?"

"The child will come to you. He is a member of a group of children called The Explorers Club. They are part of the solution. But, his faith in them is also weakening. You must make the child understand."

"But I am in no position to make anyone believe me. I am a joke to most of my flock and to the world. I can't advise anyone." He dropped his head in shame.

"God will give you the words to say and the child, he will listen. He knows your words are truthful. You will not live to see the things I show you come to pass. Know that your death will not be in vain. Those who do not believe now; will believe when you are gone. Your light will pass from your body quickly. I will not allow you to suffer. Gaze into my eyes."

Scenes flashed in the angel's eyes. Their eyes became as one. Two young boys visited the Pope then a blank space zipped by. He knew this was his death and he was not permitted to see it. Violent scenes flashed before him. He began weeping uncontrollably. The angel placed her hands on his trembling shoulders.

"The day of destruction will pass. This is not the end of time."

"Why? Why?" He repeated.

"These things must happen, when men fail to practice honesty and live or act without consciousness. Solomon Micah, hear me and obey, for your time is almost up."

The light in the room began to dim. The angel became translucent then disappeared. Pope Solomon Micah drifted into a deep peaceful sleep.

Chapter 10—MOUNT RAINIER

Mike and Tia sneaked into Polaris Labs. There weren't as many guards, now that the Pope was being labeled a lunatic. The two guards on duty were busy watching a football game. Tia and Mike crawled along the corridor. All of the security doors were open. Tia stood watch while Mike gathered the information they needed. He used the printer to print the information. Sneaking out of the building was easier than sneaking in.

Mrs. Cruz was happy to see Mike. She wished Nick was as innocent as Mike. She and her husband decided to keep Nick away from The Explorers Club. Mike and Stephanie were the only kids he would be allowed to associate with. Mike entered Nick's room.

"What are you doing here?" Nick grumbled.

"Nicholas Andropolus Cruz II," his mother growled. "You had better be nicer to your guests."

"Guests my ass!" Nick mumbled.

"What did you say, young man?" She called Nick
into the hall. Nick left his bedroom door ajar. "I've
got news for you young man. Mike is a nice young
man and you'd better get used to being around him.
Your father and I forbid you to be around Reggie and
the remaining Explorers. The Explorers Club is over
with, remember that and accept it. Mike's mother
invited you to sleep over this weekend and you're
going."

"But Mom, I can't go."

"I don't want to hear any of your excuses! You're
going Nicholas and you're going to like it!"

"I may have to go, but I don't have to like it."

Mrs. Cruz opened Nick's door shoved him in and
preceded to the kitchen. Nick closed his door. He
looked at Mike. They both fell on the bed in a fit of
laughter. Their plan had worked perfectly. After a
two-minute attack of hysteria, the boys calmed down
and began to discuss business. Mike showed Nick the
computer printouts. It revealed the I.S.S.A's plan to
have the Pope committed and a murder-suicide plan.

"We've got to get to the Pope before they succeed.
He's the one who sabotaged the project; maybe he can
help us stop the disasters."

 Nick paced the floor. He had to find a way to get to
the institution. They needed a plan, a way to keep
their parents from suspecting anything.

"Tomorrow is Saturday." Mike squealed. "I know what we can do. My parents said I could do anything I wanted for my birthday. I'll ask my Dad to take all of us camping. He can fly us to Mt. Rainier in his plane. We would be less than forty miles from the institution. I'll ask my Dad to take us to Oregon then once the plane takes off, I'll tell him we want to go to Washington, instead. If it doesn't work, I'll whine. My Dad's a sucker when I whine. Our parents will think camping will be the best thing to keep us out of trouble. If we're in the middle of the woods, how can we cause any trouble? I'm going home to set things up. Call the others and tell them to expect a call around nine." Mike thanked Mrs. Cruz for allowing him to visit and for her hospitality.

Pope Solomon Micah, still groggy from the drugs was awakened from his peaceful sleep with a jolt. Three tall green aliens were standing over him. They had large baldheads and almond shaped eyes. The shapes of their noses were normal but they didn't have nostrils. Gills protruded where ears should have been. Slimy red slits replaced their mouths. One of them put a damp cloth over his nose. He slowly drifted into darkness.

The Pope awoke in a dank smelling alley. Realizing he was in a garbage dumpster, he stood up. A car was parked at the end of the alley. He could hear the voices of two men talking. He yelled for help. Within a minute's time, a police car pulled up beside the dumpster. Officer Daly asked him what his name was. "Solomon Micah," he replied. The officer identified himself and his partner. The Pope told them about his abduction. The officers smiled, and then administered a sobriety test. When the Pope passed the test, they called downtown to their precinct.

They gave a description of Solomon Micah to the dispatcher. Five minutes later a picture flashed on their monitor. It was Solomon Micah but the name was different. The name was Micheal Breshner. He was missing from the Cascade Research Institute for the mentally insane. The police handcuffed the Pope. They drove him back to the institution.

Alex Shannon, Mike's father had gotten permission from the parents of all the children who remained in Polaris Town to take them camping. He was very pleased with his son's decision to go camping. The parents of The Explorers Club members were extremely happy. Although, the children would be together, they could cause no mischief in the middle of the woods. Everyone was packed and on the runway at eight o'clock Saturday morning. The parents said goodbye as the excited children climbed aboard the small plane. However, they didn't envy Alex Shannon. He would be spending four days and nights with seven teenagers. The plane rolled down the runway. It took off into a clear blue sky.

Alex Shannon wasn't really going to be alone with the children. He was meeting a friend near the park's entrance. Darrin Hunter was his old Navy buddy. It had been seven years since they'd seen each other. They kept in touch through emails and occasional phone calls. Mike walked to the cockpit of the plane.

"Dad," he whined. "I don't want to go to the Cascades in Oregon. I want to go to Mt. Rainier in Washington."

"But Mike, Darrin is meeting us in Oregon." His father complained.

"Can't we pick him up and take him to Washington with us? Please Dad. Besides, he lives near the Cascades in Oregon. I bet he'd like to go camping in Washington." Mike pleaded sweetly with his father.
"All right son, I'll see what I can do. We should get to Oregon before Darrin leaves the park. We'll have a big lunch and then head to Washington. How is that?"

"Dad, you're the greatest!" Mike walked happily back to his seat. He thumped Nick on the back of his head. "It's all set."

The plane landed in Oregon at eleven thirty am. They took a limo directly to Darrin's house. Darrin's wife, Samantha cooked them a lunch that looked like a feast. They ate until they felt like their stomachs would explode. Samantha was a nice friendly person. Her Spanish accent, straight red hair and dark skin made her look as strange as Mike. She and Mike looked at each other and laughed.

"I make a special snack for you." She said. "If no one catch nothing, you will still have dinner, no?"

"No," they all laughed teasingly.

They spent an extra two hours in Oregon. They hated to leave. Samantha had been wonderful. Tia and Angie Faye hugged her.

"We'll miss you."

"You come back anytime and write me, okay?"

"Okay," they smiled.

Once again, they boarded the airplane. It took off smoothly. Tia turned on the satellite TV. A special report interrupted the program.

"Hey guys, look!" She pointed to the seven-inch screen.

"This is Amy Green, reporting for the International News. Earlier today, as most of you know, Pope Solomon Micah was found to be mentally unstable at his competency trial. He was institutionalized at an undisclosed location. Since that broadcast, the religious world has turned topsy-turvy. Now, live from the Vatican City, our correspondent, Denie Marino."

"The Pope's antics have caused a major lawsuit to be launched against him and the Church. Millions are beginning to doubt their faith. It appears to me, the more hope people lose, the more violent they become. Within a few hours of our last report, crime, suicide and murder rates have doubled. Missionaries and charities are beginning to be looked upon as nuisances. A group of nuns were stoned to death less than twenty feet from the Vatican. This reporter believes a lot of worthwhile organizations are going down the drain. Thanks Pope, you've done a great job helping humanity."

Tia turned the TV off. "The world is going to turn to a pile of shit if we can't change the people's opinion of the Pope. Personally, I don't think we have a chance." The Explorers leaned back in their seats and stared out the windows helplessly. Nick wondered if The Brain was still alive.

Mrs. Bradford turned on the television. The screen was blurry but the sound was okay. Professor Norvin ran down the hall to the animal research center. He had been paged during his broadcast. Strange sounds were coming from the lab. It wasn't the typical squeaks, barks and squeals that normally greeted him. These sounds were low hoarse growls.

"What's going on Simmins?"

"The biological specimens are producing mutations. We don't know why? They haven't been injected with anything nor exposed to radiation. We are running an abundance of tests to try to find out what's going on. We should have the results tonight. I almost forgot. Dr. Vanderdaff called from the hospital. The three pregnant women all went into labor at the same time. One was in her forty-fifth week, one was post maturity and the other was only in her sixteenth week of pregnancy. The mother who was beyond her time gave birth to twins. All four babies have identical deformities and appear to be the same age. They were all in fetal distress and had to be delivered by Cesarean Section. Their faces are so distorted, the nurses are afraid of them. He also said to tell you their skin is neon green."

"What about the parents?" Professor Norvin asked.

"The parents are one hundred percent healthy. Only one couple is interspecies. They all had proper neonatal care, no history of disease or deformities and all prenatal tests were normal."

Professor Norvin's video beeper flashed. It was James Matlock, chief engineer. He asked Professor Norvin to report to the thirty-third sector near the life support systems. A tall black man was waiting near the elevator.

"Hello Professor Norvin." He pointed to a cut out section in the wall. "The metallic structures are collapsing. The areas weakened by radiation and gravity are beyond repair. We've lost fifty techs. They were trying to adjust the gyrostabilizers. According to my report, they were killed when the G-Forces became intense enough to explode their protective suits. The sound proof airlock prevented us from hearing the explosions. We didn't realize they were missing until lunch. We set off small charges to try and get them out but it was too late."

Tia and Angie Faye had pitched their tents and unrolled their sleeping bags ten minutes before the guys finished. It felt wonderful being in the mountains. It almost made them forget their troubles. Reggie and Mike hung the supplies on the limb of a large tree. They grabbed their fishing gear and headed for the lake. The temperature was cooler than usual but they were prepared for anything. Mike thought about how much fun this trip could be if the fate of the world didn't rest on their shoulders.

Alex and Darrin talked about old times. Before they knew it, the fish were cleaned and frying. The Explorers huddled together to discuss their plan.

"Chows up!" Darrin yelled. Everyone grabbed a plate and sat close to the fire. The temperature was dropping fast. Nick was famished. He ate four fish, three slices of bread and two helpings of beans. Reggie and Nick volunteered for KP. It started raining before they finished the dishes. They were drenched when they reached their tent.

The alarm on Nick's watch buzzed loudly. He had set it for two o'clock am. He and Reggie dressed quickly. They planned to sneak off and thumb a ride to the Cascade Research Institution for the mentally insane. Reggie unzipped the tent and stuck his head out. The wind was extremely cold. He zipped the tent quickly. "We're going to have a cold walk." They stuffed their sleeping bags to make it appear as if they were still sleeping. Chewing on a strip of beef jerky, they headed towards the road.

The road was dark and empty. Reggie was glad their jackets had reflective stripes. The beams from their flashlights barely scratched the darkness. Strong winds were blowing fiercely. Nick was about to say it couldn't get any worse, when he felt a cold drop of rain hit his face. The cold rain quickly turned to sleet. Gusting winds prevented them from increasing their pace.

"The best thing is to turn back while we still have a sense of direction towards the camp." Nick groaned. Light snow was blending in beautifully with the sleet. Something large ran across the road ahead of them.

"Was that a bear?" Nick asked.

"I don't know." Reggie stopped walking. "But something is coming up behind us awfully fast."

They turned to see an eighteen wheeler headed towards them. They waved their flashlights to get the drivers attention. The big truck roared past them and kept going. Their legs were like lead weights and they were tiring quickly. Reggie pulled his sleeve back to glance at his watch. Snow covered the face of his watch before he could look at it. A horn blew behind them. The driver of a large blue truck gave them the finger and kept going. One hour later, a small pickup stopped besides them. Two strange looking men were seated in the cab. The driver rolled down the window. He had long stringy hair, a thick nasty beard and he smelled badly.

"You boys want a ride." He smiled a toothless smile.

"You can sit on my lap anytime."

The other rider laughed loudly. The boys picked up their pace. The truck drove slowly besides them. The driver constantly made harassing remarks. Reggie got a brilliant idea. He told Nick to play along with him.

"Hey man," he yelled. "I don't like you but your friend is kinda cute. My friend here says if you let him drive, he'd be real grateful!"
The driver grinned. He stopped the truck, immediately. The driver leaned out of the cab.

"Pull off them hoods and let us see them pretty faces of yours." He spoke with a bad country accent. They flipped the hoods of their coats back and tried to give the men an enticing smile. The smiling men grunted, then opened the truck's doors. Nick and Reggie stepped back two feet.

"Now don't be coy, boys." The driver grinned. He stood up unzipping his pants. The boys waited until both men were on the same side of the truck. The men staggered towards the boys holding their pants up. Reggie jumped up and landed a sidekick to the driver's chin. Their Karate lessons were about to pay off. Nick kicked the other man in the groin. One more kick to their heads and the men were out cold.

The cab of the truck smelled foul. They tossed trash and liquor bottles out of the truck. Nick laid their flashlights on the floorboard. The temperature in the truck was very hot. They removed their jackets, turned on the radio and started down the highway. The digital clock read three fifteen A.M. The boys realized they hadn't been walking very long.

The roads were slippery. The boys were thankful the truck had good tires. The snow flurries increased and became larger. Nick noticed two sets of chains in the bed of the truck. They pulled into the parking lot of the institution at four thirty am. Nick removed his universal key card from his jacket pocket. "We'll go in the back way." He said. The employee's entrance was exactly where Tia said it would be.

They followed a narrow hall to the employee's dressing room. Several white uniforms were hanging in a large closet. Nick chose an orderly's uniform. Reggie put on a doctor's lab coat. The nametag read: Dr. Trenden.

"After you Doc," Nick smiled. The elevator was at the end of the hall. The doors were open. Nick pushed three. The doors closed loudly. They were nervous and feared getting caught. The elevators took less than a minute to reach the third floor. They could hear the nurses whispering from the lounge. No one was seated at the desk.

Chapter 11-FIRST SIGNS

"So far, so good." Reggie commented. He glanced at the chart on the wall. Room three hundred three would be near the end of the hallway to the left. The first door had the number three hundred twenty. They were sure the room they wanted was the one with the guard outside the door. Room three hundred three had a large sign on the door. "No Visitors!" The guard was leaning back in a chair snoring loudly. Reggie cleared his throat and stumped his foot on the floor. The guard did not stir. "Whew!" He exclaimed. Nick eased the key card into the slot. The door opened with a squeak. The guard continued to sleep. They entered the room, carefully closing the door behind them. Pope Solomon Micah was strapped to the bed. He awoke when he heard the door open.

"Who are you?" He asked.

"Quiet down!" Nick whispered. "We're not staff members. We're just kids."

"How did you get here?" The Pope asked.

"We used a universal key card and the guard being sound asleep didn't hurt." Nick smiled.

"But, what do you want?" He asked.

"We are members of a group called The Explorers Club. We live in Polaris Town. We know you have been telling the truth."

Reggie reluctantly unstrapped the Pope. He sat up so quickly that Reggie jumped back.

"I'm not going to hurt you, young man." He smiled.

Reggie and Nick sat on the floor. They told him about the message they'd received from The Brain. The Pope was brought up to date on Earthstar, the project's failure and the destruction happening around the world. Pope Solomon Micah looked weak and pitiful.

"How? How did they change the towns so fast?"

"Well," Nick said. "The buildings were constructed with a special anchor hitching that uses an interlocking modular design. The grounds were also engineered with the same consideration so that every part of the experiment could be dismantled and moved leaving no trace. The computers can shut down and recede underground where they are shielded from metal detectors. They wanted you to make a fool of yourself. They knew the public would start to question your sanity. They have also planned to force you to commit suicide or kill you and make it look that way."

"This I already know." The Pope shook his head sadly.

"We want to save our friends and the others. We need to know what you did and how to alter it," Reggie pleaded. "We will get you out of here and save your reputation."

"My time is up," the Pope smiled. "I will help you but you cannot help me. You cannot alter what is meant to be. You," he pointed to Nick. "I know you. What's your name?"

"Nick," he answered. "My father is Dr. Cruz. He's over Polaris Town."

The Pope handed Nick a small pouch. "I want you to hide this in a safe place."

"What is it?" Nick asked.

"A rainbow card, a computer disc and the code I used to alter the computers. Tell no one except your club members. Get back to Polaris and save your friends. I want you to swear in the name of the Holy Trinity that you will reveal the things you know to the public."

The boys swore to right all wrongs. "The sun is coming up; you'd better leave before the morning

crew comes in. Nick I have something to tell you."
The Pope glanced at Reggie.

"Reggie is my best friend. Whatever you have to say,
you can say in front of him." Nick remarked.

Pope Solomon Micah rubbed his face. "Your father,
he isn't a bad man and neither are the rest of us. The
Secret Under The Rainbow was supposed to be just
another experiment. We had no intention of harming
anybody. Your father loves you. He and your mother
are just trying to protect you. They are just trying to
give you the best education and a good life. Your
father could have turned his back on Polaris Labs and
took another job. It was you he was thinking of. Why
do you think he is so hard on you? He may not go
about it in the right way but he's trying. Do you
understand, Nick?"

"Yes sir. I guess I knew how my parents felt but my
anger got in the way. What they are doing to you and
the people is wrong."

"I know that Nick. But, you can't stop loving a person
because they make a mistake. I will be gone soon.
Don't let the news of my death alarm you. It is meant
to be. Now go." Reggie opened the door. The guard
jumped from his chair.

"What are we going to do?" Nick whispered.

"Who are you?" The guard demanded.

"What right do you have to question my authority?"
Reggie complained. "If you hadn't been sleeping on

the job you would have seen me enter the room. I guess you don't value your job!"

"Uh, I'm sorry sir. I really need this job. I have a wife and three kids. I promise to stay alert." The guard pleaded. "It's okay son, everyone makes a mistake. Let's go Mr. Nick."

Reggie and Nick gave a sigh of relief then entered the elevators. The parking lot was covered with snow and it showed no signs of stopping.

"It'll be after six before we get back." Reggie stated. "I hope Mike and the others can cover for us."

"The way it's snowing, I believe everyone is still in their sleeping bags." Nick laughed. "Did you see the expression on the guards face? He really thought you were a doctor."
Reggie warmed the truck up. Within a few minutes, they were back on the road. The two drunks were still out when they returned. They dragged the men over to the truck and put them in the cab. Reggie kept sniggling.

"What's so funny?" Nick asked.

"We just saved the lives of two ass holes who tried to take ours."

Reggie pulled his hand out of his pocket and dangled the truck keys in front of Nick's face. Nick laughed. He thought they should have taken the men's pants too.

When they reached the campsite, Darrin was removing the supplies from the tree limb. They hid behind a tree until Darrin went back inside his tent. They had just crawled into their tents when Darrin yelled. "It's time to get up every one!"

Alex Shannon told everyone to get packed. The weather was getting worse. It was time to go home. Everyone complained while walking down the mountain to the van. Darrin did his best to keep the van on the slick road. The children prayed and held their breath until he finally gained control of the van. They were happy to climb aboard the small plane. Darrin sat in the cockpit with Alex. He had passed out the remaining treats his wife packed. Reggie and Nick quietly told the others about their adventure. Mike briefed everyone on his next idea, how to sneak into Polaris Labs and use the rainbow computers.

The plane took off smoothly despite the ice building up on the wings. Reggie and Nick were exhausted. They slept all the way to Oregon. Samantha prepared a large breakfast. After breakfast, Tia and Angie Faye helped with the dishes. The plane took off quickly.

"On to Polaris Town," Alex Shannon told his son.

Mike glanced back. Reggie and Nick were sleeping soundly. The trip back to Polaris was silent. They all knew what had to be done.

Two astronomers from Mt. Everest were on their way to Polaris Town. They were attending an important meeting. Their analysis of Earthstar's photographs was finished. The Supersonic jet would get them to

Polaris in a few hours. They weren't looking forward to the meeting. The news they were bringing was not good. They couldn't wait for things to get back to normal, research and no emergencies.

The plane landed three hours later. Another plane landed at the same time on the opposite side of the airport. The children had seen the jet land. They climbed off the small plane and ran towards the jet. Supersonics fascinated the children. They could break the sound barrier without the audible boom. Alex Shannon remained behind unloading the plane. Nick was glad to get home. His mother had baked his favorite cookies. He apologized for the way he'd been acting and promised to try and do better.

" Mom, when will Dad be home?" He asked.

"He has an important meeting. He'll probably be gone all night." She smiled. Nick showered and crawled into bed for a nap. The Explorers were meeting at six pm. Getting past security would be impossible.

"*Unless*," he thought. " Mom! Did you say Dad would be at the labs all night?"

"No, Nick," his mother yelled. "The meeting is here in the hotel. He's going to the labs after the meeting." Mrs. Cruz entered Nick's room with an arm full of fresh linen.

"Mike invited me over to play video games, this evening." Nick yawned.

"That's great sweetheart. What time should I wake you?"

Six," Nick smiled.

"The trip worked. Maybe I can have my family back the way they were." Mrs. Cruz thought.

The conference room in Polaris Guest Hotel was packed. Armed guards were everywhere. Dr. Cruz stood at the podium.

"We are going to skip the formalities. These are the astronomers from Mt. Everest. They are Dr. Richard Weltz and Dr. William Howser. The floor is all yours gentlemen." Dr. Howser approached the podium.

"All of our findings have been checked and rechecked. We estimate at least seventy five percent of Earthstar's surfaces has been damaged. We have tried to find a solution to save as many lives as possible. The results are not very positive. The number of survivors will depend on the amount of time we have and the number of ships capable of docking." Dr. Howser yielded the floor to a technician.

"When we started these experiments, we were told Synacom 14 could withstand cruel and unusual punishments." Dr. Howser stood.

"The metal in its present state will intensify the amount of energy it absorbs. This energy will be reflected towards anything in the form of a death ray. Synacom 14 is behaving like a lens and a mirror. It's dissipating more energy than it's converting. If

Earthstar comes any closer to Earth, people may suffer blindness from viewing it with their naked eyes. I believe we will have enough time for evacuation if Earthstar's orbital changes continue to be predictable."

"If the slingshot effect continues, what will the overall effect be?" Dr. Quartz asked.

"If the planetoid changes orbits before the ships dock, we won't have to worry about saving anyone. Deep space will be their final resting place. Earthstar will collide with one of its neighbors and explode. I've told you as much as I know. It's up to you now." Dr. Cruz approached the podium.

"Thank you, Dr. Howser. Our main object is to save Earth, the people of Earthstar and salvage whatever data we can. Our solution must involve a way to stabilize Earthstar long enough for evacuation."

"I have a suggestion," Dr. Weltz said. "We will need two massive ships with additional shielding to protect the crews. Thrusters and retrorockets should get the job done."

"Thank you, Dr. Weltz." Dr. Cruz said. "We have a lot of work to do. This meeting is adjourned."

The Explorers left the hotel before the meeting started. They quietly entered the rainbow sector. The halls were quiet and intimidating. Reggie unlocked the door of the computer room. Tia and Angie Faye took turns standing guard. Nick typed the Pope's access codes in the computer. He tried without success to reverse the commands. The damage was too far gone to correct. They had made the trip for nothing. The world was still doomed and so was The Brain. They walked sadly back to the hotel. Nick cuddled on the couch beside his mother. A special report interrupted the show his mother was watching.

"Today, Pope Solomon Micah hung himself at the Cascade Research Institution for the mentally insane".

Nick sat up quickly and stared at the screen.

"He apparently tied his sheets together and threw them across a hanging incandescent light. An orderly found his body, this evening."

"There were no lights hanging in the Pope's room!" Nick yelled a little too loudly.

"What?" His mother asked.

"Nothing, I was thinking about the Pope's room in the Vatican," he lied. Nick ran upstairs.

Fighting back the tears, he crawled into bed. He wanted to call Reggie but he was sure Reggie had seen the news report too. Nick thought about their conversation with the Pope. He was glad the Pope didn't' know the codes he'd given them were no good. He wondered if the Pope had died horribly. He knew, however the Pope had died, he was at peace now.

Pam and Adam walked on a deserted beach. Adam picked up a warm shell and tossed it into the ocean. The sand was too hot to go barefoot. They wore jeans and high top tennis to protect their legs and ankles.

Walking on the beach was considered dangerous because of the intense heat.
 Pam glanced at something wriggling in the sand. Fish and other sea life were crawling out of the ocean and onto the beach to die. They were flopping and twisting frantically. A pile of dead fish washed up on the shore. Adam picked up one of the fish.

"Damn!" He yelped.

 "What's wrong?" Pam asked.

"This damn fish is scorching hot!" He picked up a pointed stick. The stick was hot but tolerable.

He stabbed the fish. The meat was coarse.

"This meat has been boiled," he said tasting the fish. Adam walked to the water's edge and inserted his hand. 'Shit!' Blisters began forming on it. "We'd better get off this damn beach."

The cool air inside the hotel felt great. Pam's head ached from the heat. She climbed on the bed and turned on the TV. Adam phoned Polaris.

"Dr. Cruz, this is Adam Stanton. I've been watching the news and I was wondering if the I.S.S.A are going to do something about this heat."

"Adam, there is so much I have to tell you but not over the phone. Find out the hotel's fax number and I'll brief you on our little situation. I need you to return to Polaris as soon as possible. We are calling all our employees back. Oh, I almost forgot. Congratulations are in order. I hope you and Pam are very happy and will be for many years to come. Please try to leave immediately after you receive my fax." Dr. Cruz said.

"Where will every one live? You removed their homes." Adam stated.

"They will live free of charge in hotels and furnished apartments in Enich Hills. I've got a meeting to attend. Do your best to return soon."

Adam told Pam to call room service and order dinner. "I have to pick up a fax. I'll explain when I return."

Adam returned fifteen minutes later with several sheets of paper. He told Pam about his conversation with Dr. Cruz. They read the fax sheets together. "Dr. Cruz wants us to return immediately. They are recalling all employees."

"But, we left to get away from the mess Polaris and the I.S.S.A created. If the world is going to be destroyed, I'd rather die here with you. This is our honeymoon. Why should we share it with Polaris and the I.S.S.A?" Pam was furious.

"Calm down, Love. I have no intention of leaving now. I told the front desk to screen all our calls. If Polaris calls, they will tell them we left at five P.M." Pam smiled and removed the covers from their food.

Chapter 12—DISASTERS!

The Brain watched the news. He and Toby were
stretched out across their makeshift beds. The news
reporter was talking about the problems the people of
Earth were having.

*"Mining operations have been halted due to cave-ins
caused by tremors. Consumers are having a hard
time paying utility bills because of rising temperatures
and the high cost of fuel. Oil wells around the Earth
have been literally bursting into flames because of the
intense heat. Others have reported unusually cold
temperatures. Volcanic activity has increased and
most of the large bodies of water have become boiling
hot. The people of Earth are praying for rain; rain
that may never come.*

*Communications of all kinds have been affected by the
intense energy waves above the Earth. The airlines
have limited flights because of problem with
compasses, altimeters, radar and electric generators.*

A pile of organic debris was found on Cuban beaches today. An unidentified policeman told news reporters the coroner's report stated the debris was the remains of several humans. Stay tuned for our local news."

The Brain turned the monitor off. The news was depressing. He had convinced himself everything on Earth was perfect. Now, he would have to face reality. Mrs. Bradford glanced tearfully through the family's photo album. She wondered if she'd ever see her husband again. She questioned whether they would live to see another day.

The television was no longer operational. She was thankful the Caniculien's monitor didn't operate off the same waves as the television. The Caniculiens were brilliant people but she hoped to leave Earthstar and never see one again. She simply wanted to go home; home to Earth with all its disasters. Charles could go to a normal public school. She and her husband could get normal jobs. Maybe he could be an airline pilot. If only God would answer her prayers and reunite her family on Earth. They had to stay healthy until the ships arrived. "The ships will come soon." She said to herself.

The Nebulas II and I were being prepared for the trip to Earthstar. Technicians were equipping two other ships with protective shielding. One of those ships would work with a Caniculien ship to help stabilize Earthstar. The other would be used to help with the evacuation process. The navigators were being briefed. The rainbow staff tried to imagine everything that could possibly go wrong. These situations were then presented to the navigators. They would have to make rash decisions in impossible situations.

Emergency supplies were stacked in the preparation room. Medical personnel were being briefed in another room. Timing was critical. The ships would only keep Earthstar stabilized for a short time. The evacuation teams would have to get in and out of the docking areas quickly. The navigators were suited with protective suits and helmets. The suits were made of spun Synacom 14. Special shielding was built into the faceplates of the helmets to protect their eyes from the dangers of radiation.

Special communication devices were installed in the ships. With these devices, communications would not be interrupted by electromagnetic interferences. The Nebula II was scheduled to depart first. It was the fastest ship the I.S.S.A owned. Its navigator's job was to reestablish contact with Earthstar. He would inform Professor Norvin of the evacuation plan. He and Professor Norvin would complete the evacuation arrangements before the other ships arrived.

Canicula and Earth had assembled emergency personnel and vehicles on their planets to prepare for the arrival of the citizens of Earthstar. Special hospitals were set up to deal with the radiation victims. All of the details had been worked out. The only thing left was to launch the ships and their crews. Dr. Cruz knew once the ships took off he would have a greater task at hand. It would be time to inform the public. There would be mass panic around the world.

The I.S.S.A established designated safety zones around the world before they started The Secret Under

The Rainbow Project. They would provide transportation to take people to their designated safety zones. The safety zones were equipped to provide shelter, food, clothing, blankets, entertainment and medical services. The shelters were underground and built of Synacom 14. The I.S.S.A had hoped they'd never have to use these shelters. It was simply supposed to be a safety precaution.

The Nebula II would lift off at fifteen hundred hours. The other ships were scheduled to launch at eighteen hundred hours. Polaris was alive with activity. Admiral Bradford climbed into the cockpit of the Nebula II. He was about to partake in the most dangerous mission of his life. The danger didn't frighten him. He was worried because his family was in the midst of a holocaust. How could he live with himself if his family died? He wondered if Charles hated him for taking him away from his peaceful life and placing him in the middle of hell.

"I may lose my job, but I'm going to make sure my family gets on the Nebula II, whether anyone else makes it or not."

The Nebula II engines hummed to life. It lifted off leaving behind a trail of fire blazing in the sky. Admiral Bradford glanced to his left. Once again Earthstar appeared in the skies above Polaris Town. The trip was almost over. In less than thirty minutes he would be communicating with Earthstar. Although the trip only took a few hours, he felt as if he'd been traveling for days. Twenty minutes later, he removed a card with Morse code on it from his pocket.

This is the Nebula II please respond.

The response came immediately.

This is Professor Norvin go ahead.

I am the first of eight ships. Canicula and Earth are sending six ships for evacuation. We realize the problem you are having with stability. Therefore, we will use two ships to try and maintain stability while we proceed with the evacuation.

Professor Norvin responded again.

Six ships will not be capable of docking at the same time. It would cause a major upset. I suggest two ships at a time, one from each planet. Earth can use dock A and Canicula can use dock B. Docks E thru G have collapsed. All the people are in the safety areas of their homes. I will try to arrange for different sectors to go to the docking areas one at a time. When will the other ships arrive?

Admiral Bradford responded.

They will arrive in two hours or less. Tell the people to leave all their belongings behind. We will have what they need on the ships. Medical staffs are also available. What percent of the population are we talking about evacuating?

Professor Norvin answered.

Less than two thirds of the population are still alive. I suggest we remove the healthy people and let the others die. A lot of them are beyond help.

This frightened Admiral Bradford.

What about my family?

Professor Norvin smiled and responded.

They are in sector ten. They are fine. I will start making arrangements now.

Wait, the Admiral responded. *Have my family brought to the docks immediately. I am now positioning the Nebula II for docking. The rest of the people can wait until the other ships are in place.*

The monitor made a loud humming noise. Mrs. Bradford glanced up. Professor Norvin's face appeared on the monitor.

"Our home is in its final hours. I don't want you to panic because help is on the way. I've received a message from the Nebula II less than twenty minutes ago. Canicula and Earth are sending fourteen ships to rescue us."

He thought lying about the number of ships would keep the people from panicking.

"This will be more than enough transportation. The sick will be loaded first. I will then call you sector by sector. I want you to proceed to the docks in an orderly fashion. There is no need to panic. I realize you have seen the structures falling around you, but we have ample time to evacuate everyone. We will only be using docks A and B. I will announce the ships arrival and what sectors the trams will carry."

Professor Norvin left the studio. He sat a large crystal desk in his office. Cynnia, he told his secretary, get the infirmary on the line. Five minutes later, he was speaking with the administrator.

"Kill all the remaining patients and have your staff report to their homes." The professor demanded.

"But they don't all have radiation sickness. Some have viruses and other problems." The administrator said.

Just kill them all and go home!" Professor Norvin said.

Toby jumped. A loud knock on the security doors echoed throughout the house.

"Who's there?" Mrs. Bradford asked nervously.

"Earthstar guard patrol." A deep voice responded. Mrs. Bradford opened the door.

"Mrs. Bradford?" The man asked.

"Yes," she responded.

"Is this your family?" The man asked.

"Yes," she said. "Then come with us." He gestured.

"What is this about?" Mrs. Bradford asked. "Our badges are not green."

"Yes, I know ma'am. Just please come quietly." The guard pointed to Toby.

"Is that your son?" Mrs. Bradford didn't know whether to answer yes or no? She didn't want to endanger Toby's life but she didn't want to leave him behind. The Brain spoke up.

"Yes, this is my little brother." The guard ushered them out the door.

A mini tram had backed up to the living room door. A clear enclosed walkway had been installed between the back of the mini tram and the front door. They were handed protective clothing. The guard told them to dress quickly. Artificial air was blowing through the walkway.

"They don't want us to breathe the air." The Brain whispered. Brain and Toby took seats by the windows.

They wanted to see what was happening in the world outside. The artificial sky was no longer blue with white puffy clouds. It was neon orange with black and gray white clouds. Beams from sector walls had fallen on some of the houses. Two guards in protective clothing were hoarding people like cattle into the back of a large truck with chains across the doors.

The radiation badges, the people were wearing glowed like neon green flashlights. Some of them were fighting. Others just accepted their fate. The Brain knew these people would not live long enough to reach their home planets.

A garbage truck drove slowly down the street. Toby noticed they were not collecting garbage. Orange beams of light lifted the bodies and tossed them into the back of the truck. Toby and The Brain had become immune to the horrid sights of Earthstar. They glanced at each other and then stared blankly out the windows. Toby pointed to a glowing light in the thirty-third sector. A tear formed in The Brain's eye.

"The life support systems are going to explode. Earthstar is doomed. I don't know what they are going to do with us, Toby. But, according to the direction we are traveling; I'd say we are headed for the docks."

The mini tram stopped at the entrance of the docking areas.

"Go to the end of dock A and wait." The guard pointed to a sign. Dock A flashed constantly. A buzzing sound came from the sign. Sparks popped from the sign and the sign fizzled out. Toby looked up at the guard. "

Aren't you coming with us?"

"No, now go." He yelled sternly.

The tunnel which led to dock A was long and narrow. Toby looked back. The guards were gone. Most of the squiggly lights in the tunnel had burned out. They imagined all kinds of hideous creatures waiting for them at the end of the tunnel. The Brain imagined a Caniculien firing squad. The firing squad would give them a choice. They had the option of being shot or drifting forever in open space. He pictured the three of them jumping off the docks. The zero gravity would send their blood pressure soaring so high their heads would explode.

Toby imagined his mother standing at the end of the dock with his father. His mother had no head. She stood there with a knife cutting at wrists that were no longer there. His father had turned green. His skin was dripping off his body. Part of his skull was exposed. They were both reaching for him.

Mrs. Bradford envisioned a man standing ahead of them in a protective suit. The children ran towards the man for help. The man lifted them in the air and crushed their bodies together. She could see herself standing there staring at a puddle of red mush that had once been Toby and her son. She grabbed her mouth. Her daydream was coming true. A man in a protective suit stood eighty feet ahead of them. The boys ran to the man asking for help. She tried to warn the boys but the only sound that came from her mouth was a whimper.

The man lifted both boys in the air. The boys shrieked. He squeezed them against his chest. She wanted to run and protect them but her feet were frozen with fear. Suddenly, she realized the boys were not shrieking with pain. They were laughing. She looked at the man holding the children. He was hugging them not crushing them. The man removed his faceplate. It was Robert.

"Oh God; It's Robert!" She ran to him. "I knew you would come." They embraced for a few seconds.

"We've got to get aboard the Nebula II quickly." He told them. "I had to make sure you were saved first."

The Nebula I, the Zoltaire and a monstrous ship called Tor were less than one hour from Earthstar. Four Caniculien ships were also speeding towards Earthstar. Earthstar shook spasmodically and dropped further out of orbit.

An unknown employee was chosen to represent the I.S.S.A at the press conference. Kenny Robinson was a token employee. He was hired to show the world that the I.S.S.A hired people other than geniuses to work in their laboratories. Kenny barely finished high school. During the nineties, he was no more than a bum on the streets. He sold drugs for a living. Most drug dealers in those days made hundreds even thousands of dollars. But poor Kenny had to supplement his income with food stamps.

He lived from ghetto to ghetto. In nineteen ninety-eight, Kenny had six children. By the year two thousand three, he had ten children spread throughout the tri-state area. His luck changed when drugs were eliminated and ghettos banished. He tried being a hit man for a while but he was too big of a coward to continue. Tired of looking over his shoulders, he climbed the barbed wire fence around Polaris Town. He was found the next morning asleep behind a trashcan. Kenny was fortunate because government inspectors were coming to the town to see if any employees were ranked less than genius. He was swept off his feet and hauled into the showers. A foreign stranger asked him if he would like a job.

Kenny wasn't really looking for a job he just wanted a handout. The man told him he could make more money than he'd ever dreamed of making. Kenny asked what kind of work was involved.

"I don't be doing no hard work," he told the man.

"Oh, you will barely be working at all. You will clean cages, feed the animals, run errands and whatever else comes up." The foreign man smiled. "Your job title will be lab technician 1. We will pay you seven hundred a week to start."

"Hey man, like I'll take it." Kenny said. "You know man, you all right."

 The shower was filthy. The doors opened to reveal a naked but clean Hispanic about thirty-five years old. The stranger quickly dressed him in a white shirt and pants. A lab coat would be added as soon as they made him a nametag and badge. Three hours later, you would have thought Kenny had been there for years. He wasn't ignorant; he'd just never tried to accomplish anything. The I.S.S.A got past the government inspection and Kenny had ambition for the first time in his life.

"No more trash cans, no more ghetto bitches, I am going to have a decent life style."

Kenny made this promise to himself. He made plans daily. He achieved all of his goals except one. He wanted to marry a descent girl and raise a family. Maria Sanchez was going to be that lucky lady. She and Kenny had been dating for years. He was so busy being briefed on the press conference that he couldn't get away long enough to buy her an engagement ring.

This press conference was very important to him. The I.S.S.A believed in him enough to trust such an important task to him. They were going to increase his salary and give him a five hundred thousand dollar bonus. A limo picked him up and drove him to the only television station still operating. The station was in Bowling Green, Kentucky.

He was very proud. His face would be seen on television worldwide. Poor Kenny never realized the I.S.S.A was just using him. It felt good to have an idiot on their team. They were thinking of hiring more in the future.

Nick lay across his bed watching a special news report. "What a crap of shit." He thought. "They're only telling half of the truth. Somehow, I knew they'd pin all the blame on the Pope. Heaven must be spectacular because good men go through a lot of hell to get there." Nick angrily turned the television off and tossed the remote control against the wall.

A new attitude had engulfed the world since the Pope's death. The I.S.S.A emergency broadcast about a planetoid falling towards Earth only made the situation worst. All over the globe people were screaming with terror and disbelief. Violence, looting and death had become a daily event. Preparations were being made for the inevitable evacuation. The fear of an invasion of little green men had been greatly exaggerated by the public.

People were arming themselves to fight an enemy they had never seen. The threat of violence didn't panic everyone. Storeowners and businesses were ecstatic. People were buying food; camping equipment, clothing, blankets, weapons, medicinal supplies and other items they felt were essential for their survival. The demands were far exceeding the supplies.

Credit card companies denied everyone. The economy was falling apart but no one cared. They continued to close all bank accounts and cash in their investments. The stores were only accepting cash. All those who couldn't buy what they wanted, stole it. The stock market crash of nineteen twenty nine was about become reality again. The hospitals were flooded with requests from pregnant women to induce their labor early. The majority of the women who were four months pregnant or less turned to abortions. Animals were being purchased in large numbers. Animals reacted to radiation quicker than humans. Their behaviors changed when they felt threatened and their symptoms appeared quicker.
People around the world flooded the I.S.S.A and government offices with calls about the safety zones. They wanted to go to the nearest safety zone ahead of time. To keep down panic, their requests were being met. The interstates and highways were crowded with people trying to get to safety zones. Wrecks and fights were a common sight. Everyone realized the worst was yet to come. Earthstar now appeared above the Earth as often as the rising sun. The majority of the I.S.S.A employees had returned to work. The I.S.S.A had deliberately waited for their employees to get where they were going before making their announcement to the public.

They knew the public would panic and the highways and airports would become congested. People had to pay outrageous prices to fly from one place to another. Prices were drastically higher if their destinations were farther away. The I.S.S.A towns were equipped with radiation free safety zones. Only employees and their families were allowed in these safety zones.

Adam and Pam had not returned to Polaris Town. They were kept on top of the situation through faxes. The highways were too chaotic to risk a trip home. Dr. Cruz planned to fly them to Polaris Town as soon as possible. Polaris' two helicopters were on their way back to the lab. He'd estimated their time of arrival to be in four hours.

Pam wasn't exactly thrilled with the idea of returning to Polaris Town. Although the safety zones were the best place for them, she couldn't shake the feelings of disaster and doom.

"Nick... Nick had been right all the time." Why hadn't she listened to him? "Maybe, a lot of this could have been avoided. Oh Nick, I'm sorry. The world is about to be destroyed because I didn't have the courage to follow my own thoughts."

"My family, I wonder if they've left for the safety zones." Pam picked up the phone. She dialed her sister's house. Her family and Adam's family had left Gulf Port, Mississippi immediately after the wedding. Leitha answered on the second ring.

"Leitha are you all right?" Pam asked.

"Sure Pam, our designated safety zone is less than two miles from the house. We're going to leave once it gets dark. Some of the traffic would have eased up by then." Leitha yawned.

"You're not taking the car, are you?" Pam
questioned.

"No we're using the Jeep. We will be able to avoid
the highway and take a short cut across the fields.
We've packed our food and supplies. We'll be fine.
What are you and Adam going to do?"

"Well," Pam hesitated. "We're going back to Polaris
Town."

"Driving?" Her sister questioned.
"No," Pam comforted. "Polaris is sending a
helicopter for us." The phone line began to pop.
"We'd better hang up, Pam the static is horrible. I
love you and I'll see you when this crisis is over.
Goodbye Pam."

"Goodbye Leitha, I love you too." Pam cried.
Someone knocked on their door. Adam opened the
door.

"Room service," a young man smiled. Adam knew
the red faced teen wore a clown's face. Underneath
the fake smile, the boy was worried. Adam handed
him an extremely large tip. The boy handed the
money back to Adam.

"Thanks, but it has no value." The tall curly haired
boy rubbed his hands through his thick red hair. "I'm
leaving in a few minutes. My parents are coming to
get me. My boss said he'd fire me if I leave. But
what difference does that make? If I am gonna die,
I'd rather be with my family. If I could get my hands
on the I.S.S.A and its employees, I'd kill them. I got
a gun you know. They ruined it for us. I'm just a kid

and my life is over. My sister had an abortion this morning. She has been trying to get pregnant for six years. When she finally makes it, she has to get rid of it. She doesn't want to give birth to a radioactive monster. The I.S.S.A is still hiding something. They aren't telling the complete truth. My grandparents were visiting Sweden for their fiftieth anniversary. Some anniversary it turned out to be. They both died of radiation sickness yesterday. My grandparents were healthier than most twenty year olds. I gotta go," he cried.

Tears ran down the young man's face. The door slammed shut behind him. Neither Pam nor Adam could speak. Adam reached for the remote control.

"A little television should cheer us up."

Pam sadly picked at her food. She wondered if their lives were in danger. If that young man wanted to kill I.S.S.A employees, imagine how many other people are thinking the same thing. Several people in the hotel knew they were I.S.S.A employees. It would not take long for information like that to spread.

She imagined people with clubs trying to break down their door. She and Adam would have to climb out the window on sheets they'd tied together.

"Snap out of it," Adam smiled. Adam was watching the comedy hour. His favorite comedian was on. Pam smiled. Instantly, she became engrossed in the comedian. Her fish, French fries and slaw began to taste wonderful.

"I am hungrier than I thought." She finished her tea and began drinking Adam's tea. Outside, Earthstar continued to fall closer to Earth. A man glanced out his window. He saw a large glowing ball growing larger and larger. He realized the thing he was looking at was Earthstar.

"That's the thing everyone's making all that fuss about."

He stood at the window staring at the huge planetoid. It made him think about the close up shots of the Earth sent back from satellites. It was a beautiful scene.

"I wish Martha could have been alive to see this. She would have thought it was right pretty."

The old man continued to stare out of his window. "It's absolutely breathtaking. God, it's spectacular. It's so close. I bet I could fly out the window and land there. If I look close enough I bet I could see the people there."

The thought of actually seeing the people of Earthstar frightened him. He wanted to step away from the window, but the giant mural of Earthstar had mesmerized him. This amazing scene was the last thing he would ever see. A golden ray of light zipped across the sky from Earthstar into the man's living room.

The man never realized what was happening to him. The golden ray touched him and he exploded into a pile of ashes. Electrical appliances and light fixtures around the world began to blink. People watched the intensified heat rays with awe. The rays were similar to sun beams, only wider and more powerful. Golden rays burned fields, houses and killed those that it touched. Airplanes flying near the rays exploded scattering debris and body parts for miles. A ray flashed against a glass mirrored building in Dallas Texas.

The ray reflected off the building and onto a hospital. No one survived. The I.S.S.A instructed its towns around the world to enter their safety zones. Soldiers and guards were assigned to the I.S.S.A vehicles. The people would need protection from themselves as well as rioters and looters. The trucks, buses and vans were to be boarded in an orderly fashion. Panic would only cause injury and death. It would not be tolerated.

WRGB was now the only television station broadcasting. Bernard Lancaster was preparing for a special news bulletin. He had been WRGB's anchorman for five years. If the world survived its collision with Earthstar he would finally get the promotion he'd been waiting for. Marvin Branch, the station manager moved to another state. Bernard had dreamed about being station manager for years.

"How bad can my luck be? I finally get the chance to move up and the fucking world decides to end."

"It's time," the producer yelled. Bernard adjusted his microphone. He sat behind a circular blue and white desk. The red light on the camera glowed. Background music began to play softly. The producer counted down. "Five, four, three, two, one, we're rolling."

*"We interrupt your regular programming for a special
news bulletin. Good afternoon, I'm Bernard
Lancaster and this is a WRGB news special.
Government officials have ordered military guards to
assist evacuation teams. The trucks and buses are
not arriving fast enough to avoid mass hysteria.*

*People have been trampling one another when the
trucks arrive. Guards have tried unsuccessfully to stop
people from pulling passengers out of the rescue
vehicles. The panicky behavior of people is causing
families to be separated on the buses and trucks.
Frantic and uncaring strangers running for their lives
have trampled terrified children separated from their
families.*

*Volunteers and paramedics attempting to aid the
injured are becoming victims themselves. The world
may be in turmoil, but we don't have to turn against
each other. Fighting is acceptable when we have
intelligent reasons to justify the violence. So why are
we fighting each other now? I realize we are all
feeling helpless but these senseless acts of violence
will not solve our problems. The time has come for
us to gather strength and rediscover the meaning of
brotherhood. If we help each other the evacuation
process will be smoother and faster.*

*Now, I'd like to go to our correspondent in London,
England. Carrey Franklon are you there?"*

"Yes Bernard", he said.

*"Could you bring us up to date on your situation there
please?"* Bernard fumbled the papers on his desk.

"Well, Bernard," Carrey said. *"Buildings are collapsing, water mains and gas lines are rupturing because of earthquakes and other natural disasters. Only those who are able to walk out of collapsing buildings are being taken to the safety zones. There is no time to dig through the rubble to search for survivors. Therefore, they are being left to die. As you can see behind me, fires and explosions are all around us. The radiation is acting as a silent assassin. It maims those that it hasn't mercy enough to kill.*

Cataracts, lesions, sores, hemorrhages and dehydration plague not only the poor but also the rich. Living skeletons are beginning to walk the streets. The radiation sickness is not prejudiced. It chooses everyone. There are too many patients and not enough doctors to treat them. Hundreds have died from food and water contamination. People are literally walking over the dead lying in the street. A lot of people will never make it to the safety zones because of the traffic jams, rocks bricks and homemade bombs being catapulted at government vehicles. Rioters are trying to get even with the people who caused this destruction. They realize they'll die if they don't get to the safety zones but they are too full of anger and hate to care.

Ministers are holding prayer meetings while awaiting transportation to the safety zones. They are praying for us and crying for the generations to come. There is so much debris that the I.S.S.A vehicles are having trouble traveling to and from the safety zones. Sometimes people have to jump out of vehicles to avoid falling debris. Roads are blocked and detours

*are taking people miles from their destinations.
Fallen power lines are creating blackouts.   When
night comes visibility is almost impossible.   Back to
you, Bernard."*

*"We have reports from all over the globe about
Earthstar's death rays.   The people of Earth are now
feeling the full wrath of Earthstar.   Its death rays are
already leaving ashes and scorched flesh as far as the
eye of man can see.
Gazing at green fields on the side of the highway used
to be a travelers favorite pastime.   Now the only
scenery is lifeless barren land.   Livestock are dying in
the pastures by the thousands.   Earthstar's death
rays, starvation and contamination are taking their
toll on all the animals.   Food and water can no
longer be taken for granted; they will need to be tested
before consumption.
 The only supplies deemed reasonably safe are the
ones stored in the safety zones underground.
Emergency sirens are beginning to sound.   Around
the world people are suffering from violent mobs,
mudslides and other natural disasters.   Yesterday an
imperfect world and today we are trying to cope with
the reality of annihilation of an entire world.   This is
Bernard Lancaster reporting for WRGB.   We promise
to keep reporting the news as long as this station
remains on the air."*

Adam received a cryptic message from Dr. Cruz.   The
hotel they were staying in would be hit by one of
Earthstar's rays within the hour.   They would have to
evacuate immediately.   Adam called the front desk
and asked the hotel manager to warn their guests.

"I am preparing to leave now. If the guests are warned now we may all have a chance to survive."

"What about your bill?" The manager asked. "If you want me to pay it, you'd better have it up here in three minutes. You won't have time to collect everyone's bills before the hotel disintegrates."

"No one leaves my hotel without paying!" The manager was cross.

"Please just warn the people," Adam said.

"Yeah, right." The manager slammed the receiver down.

"Pam, I don't think he is going to warn anyone." Adam dropped his head.

"Then we'll warn them," she said.

"But we don't have time to warn them." Adam sighed.

"Oh yes we do. Just grab what we need to take with us. When do we rendezvous with the helicopter?" She smiled.

"In a few minutes and less than a mile away," He said.

Pam knocked on the doors next to their room. "Tell everyone this hotel is about to be destroyed by Earthstar. We have less than an hour to get out."

She and Adam knocked on several doors. They also stood in the hallways and yelled. They went floor by floor yelling of the impending doom. People began running from the hotel. They looked like frightened animals during a forest fire. Adam cranked up the car.

Within ten minutes a beam of light disintegrated the hotel. The hotel glowed white and then it was gone. Earthstar's rays were becoming more and more destructive. The closer it came to Earth, the stronger its rays became. The world was starting to look like a barren wasteland. Vegetation no longer existed. Rivers and other bodies of water were evaporating but the water no longer fell to the Earth as rain. The land was drying and cracking.

Pam watched the destructive rays burn cars white then explode or disintegrate them. "The end is here." She thought. Adam parked the car in the middle of an open field. A black helicopter with the words Polaris Town written on the side of it came into view. The wind from the helicopter nearly blew them off their feet. They climbed onboard the helicopter and buckled their seat belts. The pilot was a friend of theirs.

His name was Wayne Hilliard. Wayne flew his first helicopter at the age of nine. His father was an airplane mechanic whose hobby was building and flying helicopters. As a child Wayne knew more about helicopters than most pilots learned in a lifetime. "I got here in the nick of time." He said pointing to a mob across the field. They were heavily armed.

"You guys will get an aerial view of the destruction."

"Wayne, do you still have that six inch TV?" Adam asked.

"Yeah its back there with Pam," he answered. Pam passed the small satellite TV to Adam. Adam wanted to see what Bernard Lancaster was saying about the disasters. The small TV fizzled then a soap commercial appeared on the screen.

Wayne pointed to the ocean. All kinds of marine life floated on top of the ocean. It looked like everything in the ocean was dead. On the ground they saw angry people blowing up buildings and cars. Fires were everywhere. Wayne flew lower. They watched people pull others from their cars. They were killing each other for transportation to the safety zones. No one seemed to have the patience to wait for the I.S.S.A buses and vans.

The world was becoming a dusty war zone. Adam glanced at the TV. Bernard Lancaster's face was staring back at him.

"Turn up the sound, please," Pam asked. Bernard Lancaster wiped his forehead with a handkerchief. The air conditioner in the building was no longer functioning.

"Many people feel they can't trust the I.S.S.A to provide shelters and supplies for them. So they are refusing to go to the safety zones. Most of them are looking for places they think are safe. One woman told us she was taking her families into the mountains. A man told us the caves were the only safety zones. The clouds have become thicker around the Earth. The temperature as you know has become unbearable.

*Earthstar no longer shares and orbit with the moon.
It is now free to spiral towards the Earth on a
collision course with death. That's it for right now.
We will return with an update in one hour if it's
possible."*

Pam glanced back at the ocean. Two tankers filled
with crude oil exploded simultaneously. Earthstar's
hot rays had struck again. The debris and flames
could be seen for miles. Pam didn't think anyone was
really watching.

She watched a small convoy of I.S.S.A trucks below
them. The trucks stopped several times to remove
small trees and other debris from the road. They
swerved to avoid large trees and other debris they
could not move. Pam was so engrossed in the scene
it scared her when Adam touched her arm.

"Put on your parachute and hurry." He said.

"Wh-What is it?" She stammered.

"We've got to bail out!" He said. "The ray is
heading towards us. We'll be safer on the ground."

"Why can't we just land?" Pam asked.

"Wayne is going to try but just in case we have to jump before he lands, we'd better be prepared."

Pam slipped into her parachute. Their parachutes were connected to silver reflective jackets. The parachutes were also reflective. Pam hoped the rays would bounce off of them since they were made of spun Synacom 14. The helicopter started to descend. They could see Earthstar's rays heading directly towards them. Wayne adjusted his parachute. Adam kicked the helicopter doors open. A small airplane flew between them and the oncoming ray.

Chapter 13—OMEGA, THE END

A handsome young man sat behind the wheel of an I.S.S.A truck. He was thinking of a conversation he and his wife had seven months ago. He wanted to become a father as soon as possible. Charlie had disagreed quickly. She said she wanted to adjust to Carlos and marriage before planning a family. They also needed a better job. He wanted to go back to school but his job took up most of his time. He knew if he got a better job, Charlie would see things his way.

Carlos began working for the I.S.S.A two months after their conversation. Three months after he began his new job, Charlie was pregnant. He stared at the nightmarish scenes through his windshield. He wondered if his thoughts had been rational.

Burning houses lined both sides of the street. Mobs were attacking people trying to board vehicles. He blew his horn at the mobs. A blazing apartment building collapsed covering the mobs. Bricks flew in all directions. The unsuspecting tenants were on their balconies waiting for I.S.S.A vehicles to arrive. Some of them died without uttering a cry. Two blocks ahead of the trucks, a section of the interstate collapsed. The sound of honking horns echoed throughout the streets. Carlos slammed his foot on the brakes. It would be hard but he intended to avoid further catastrophes. An angry mob came out of nowhere and open fired on the people in back of his truck.

They pulled the bodies out of the truck and took their places. The idea of guards riding shotgun didn't frighten them. To them the guards were simply taking up space. They had to go too. It was the same with I.S.S.A vehicles around the world. Not one driver had been injured. The mobs understood only the drivers could get them to the safety zones.

A searing hot mist that looked like a cottony fog descended below the horizon. Several trucks ran into ditches. Drivers whose windows were down, lungs burned and suffocated from inhaling the mist. Some of their passengers suffered blindness. Many of the trucks burst into flames. The flames and smoke were almost invisible through the mist.

Carlos turned on the lights of his truck. The illumination emitted by the bulbs was eerie. The road and everything ahead of them became crystal clear. Carlos heard a loud roar overhead. A bright flash of light and a loud explosion sounded. Flight two fourteen had exploded in midair. Simultaneously, two more explosions sounded. Hot metal and organic debris fell from the sky like rain. Carlos made a right turn and joined the other trucks.

A strange beam of gold light flashed in the direction he had just left. Everything vanished. Carlos wanted to hurry and rendezvous with the other trucks. They were called the S-Side Company. The trucks approached a small town. The town was dark. There were no streetlights or neon signs. Not even a flashlight could be seen. "I've got to keep my eyes peeled for trouble," Carlos thought.

The other drivers were having the same thoughts. The area was silent. The drivers had seen several disaster areas but nothing was as eerie as this town. This town was desolate. There were no bodies, animals or plants in sight. They wanted to stop but they were afraid Earthstar would catch up with them. In the midst of the darkness, a small light glowed from the window of an obscure structure.

"There's a light on in this God forsaken place. Someone must be here. We've got to stop."

Carlos honked his horn twice. This was the signal to stop. Radio communication was no longer possible. The drivers put their protective helmets on. They hoped Earthstar was causing destruction elsewhere. Passengers were instructed to remain in the trucks. The door of the structure was unlocked. One of the men yelled. His voice echoed through the small structure. They searched around corners, under debris and behind several doors. One door opened to reveal a metal staircase heading into what appeared to be a cellar.

The men walked down the steps through a labyrinth of winding tunnels. One of them marked the walls to avoid getting lost. When they finally reached the end of the maze; they saw a large metallic door with a small window. An array of flashing lights and switches lined the walls of the narrow room. One of the men brushed against a lighted panel near the door. It was an electronic lock.

Scott Worthington was the perfect man to decode the lock. He could crack cryptographic codes and perform an alarming number of permutation equations at the same time. He asked the men to be as quiet as possible. He listened to the tone of the buttons. Twenty seconds later the lock played a familiar tune. The door opened slowly. In the far left corner of the room, a bloody and half delirious man was slumped against the wall. Carlos kneeled beside the man.

"We are a rescue team sent to evacuate citizens to the safety zones."

 The glassy eyed man stared at them. He smiled a toothless smile and began speaking in a broken dialect.

"So, you tink you can rescue somebody, do ya? I might as well tell ya. I know who you is. You from dat S-Side comp-nee. Your ain't gonna make it."

Silence filled the room. The men pondered the stranger's words. One of them conjured up the nerve to ask the stranger a question he already knew the answer too.

"What do you mean we won't make it?"

The old man said nothing. The frightened driver kneeled on one knee. He grabbed the frail little old man by the collar. He yelled and pleaded for an answer to his useless question. The old man smiled.

"Teams wit yo letters carry de dead," he grinned. "De people are marked and so are you. De I.S.S.A sent you here knowing dat de mobs would kill you." The old man coughed up a wad of blood. "Evacuation teams all over de world got yo letters. S-Side, don't you get it? It means suicide." The man was interrupted by a loud rumbling sound.

"Is there another way out of here?" Carlos asked. The old man gagged. "Push de blue button off to itself on de right wall."

Carlos obeyed the old man's instructions. The wall opened to reveal the outside world. They laid the old man on a blanket. They gently lifted and carried the makeshift stretcher to the trucks.

"We are going to beat the odds, old man." Carlos said. He instructed the men to put the old man in the cab of his truck.

"What happened here?" He asked cranking the truck.

"My name is Dodd Olsen," The old man croaked. Carlos handed him a canteen of water.

"Wet your throat." The name snapped in his mind.

"*The* Todd Olsen? What are you doing out here?" Todd took a deep breath and began to explain.

"De I.S.S.A tried to destroy dat blamed planetoid. Dey weren't gonna tell de folks about it. Dey used a parabolic mirrored doohickey to try and change de magnetic field around Earthstar. Dey hoped it would push dat booger away from Earth and back where it came from." Todd laughed. "Dat dang planetoid changed dat energy into radiation and throwed it right back here in Prospect Corners. It made one of dem dare worm holes appear and killed thousands of people for miles around."

"Why weren't you killed along with the others?" Carlos asked.

"Well," Todd coughed. "My home was designed long before Synacom 14 came to be. I designed it myself. It's completely safe from radiation."

The trucks drove as quickly as possible. The drivers had to be very cautious. There was still a lot of debris on the roads. They had to stop because of a large hole in the ground five miles outside of town. Carlos and the other drivers removed a large silver disc from the side of the road. They placed it over the hole. The drivers entered their trucks and continued their dangerous journey. They never realized a lone figure lay at the bottom of the hole in a drainpipe.

Carlos was thinking about his wife. She was waiting for him in Polaris Town's safety zone. As he entered the gates of Polaris Town, Todd Olsen inhaled for the last time. The trucks were sent away from Polaris Town. They were told to take the people to the next safety zone on their route.

The zone was twenty miles away. Carlos left the
body of Todd Olsen outside Polaris Town's gates.

It took the trucks two hours to reach their destination.
There were no buildings or cars in sight. The people
wondered if they were to roam in the woods. Carlos
removed a small key card from his pocket. He
pushed it into the crack of a large rock extending from
a hillside. He turned the rock in a forty-five degree
angle. The people heard a loud rumble. The side of
the hillside slid open to reveal a large staircase. Tiny
incandescent lights illuminated the stairs. The
staircase led deeper into the hillside. Slowly, the
hillside closed behind them.

The safety zone had one large bedroom. There was
an entertainment room with video games, pool tables
and other recreational items. A smaller room next to
the entertainment room was the observation room for
the technicians. The techs had separate living
quarters. There were numerous bathrooms and a large
cafeteria. The people were given name tags and
assigned sleeping carts. The truck drivers left their
passengers behind and headed back to Polaris Town's
safety zone. Their safety zone was larger and more
luxurious than the other safety zones.

Nick sat at his computer. He had been in the same
spot for more than five hours.

"That's it!" He yelled. "I knew it. Dad. Dad!"

Dr. Cruz was packing his luggage. He wanted their
suites in the safety zones to be as similar as possible to
their homes.

"What is it Nicholas?" He asked. "I'm busy."

"The safety zones aren't completely safe." Nick yelled. His father grimaced.

"What are you talking about?"

"Although Synacom 14's natural properties resist radiation; it does not have the converter generators or the freedom to move as Earthstar does. The stationary targets will be exposed to constant threats of earthquakes, aftershocks, Earthstar's rays and the nuclear fallout when the computers explode. The builders didn't take all of this into consideration, because Earth has an atmosphere. They probably thought Earthstar would explode far enough from Earth to avoid endangering Earth and its inhabitants. Admit it Dad. They neglected to figure the amount of stress and pressure the explosion would have on the Earth's crust, mantle and tectonic plates as well as the durability of Synacom 14."

"I realize you are very smart Nicholas and I applaud that. But, you're trying to knock the research it took brilliant minds years to develop. You've spent a few hours at a computer. I'm sorry son, but you are wrong. The safety zones are simply that, safety zones. Now get packed and I'll meet you there later. You've got twenty minutes to get to the safety zone."

Nick phoned Reggie. He told him to call the remaining Explorers and meet him at his house. The Explorers gathered in Nick's room. He explained why the safety zones were dangerous.

"Where can we go?" Mike asked.

"We need to go to the caverns." Nick gestured.

"The caves don't have Synacom 14." Tia stated.
"It doesn't matter. They are deep in the ground. The deeper they are the safer they are. If the safety zones had been deeper in the ground, they would be safe. We don't have time to discuss the flaws in the safety zones. Are you with me or not?" Nick asked.

The Explorers took Dr. Cruz's sports utility vehicle from the hotel garage and headed for the caves. The caves were normally a forty-five minutes' drive but with the condition of the roads and fields it took them nearly three hours. They watched the destruction and violence along the roads. Reggie sat quietly gripping his father's semi-automatic rifle. He hoped he'd never have to use it.

Angie Faye had packed canned goods and bottled water. Max brought a portable radio and a battery operated refrigerator filled with food. Steffie brought blankets, sleeping bags and tools. The Explorers tried to gather everything they figured necessary. Tia prayed Earthstar would not explode before they made it to their destination. A mob blocked the road ahead of them.

"What are we going to do?" Tia asked.

"We're gonna gun this sucker." Reggie smiled.

He stomped his foot on top of Nick's and forced it to the floor. They hit the mob with such force that bodies flew everywhere. The Explorers sighed a remorseful relief. They did what had to be done to save their lives. Reggie tried to make light of the situation but he felt just as bad as the others.

They parked below the entrance to the caverns. The caverns descended hundreds of miles below sea level. The Explorers had no intention of going down that deep. A loud explosion echoed throughout the caves. Dr. Cruz's precious truck had been destroyed. Earthstar's deadly rays had struck again. They never looked back. The Explorers took a deep breath and continued their descent deeper into the caverns. The remainder of their walk was silent.

The citizens of Earthstar watched their monitors closely and silently. Professor Norvin addressed the people.

"We have finally reestablished contact with the ship from Earth. There are several Earth and Caniculien ships orbiting Earthstar. Because of all the problems we are having, they can only dock two at a time. I assure you there are enough ships and enough time to evacuate the entire population of Earthstar. I will instruct you sector by sector to go to the docking areas when the ships arrive. If we proceed in an orderly manner everyone will be capable of boarding the ships safely. Earthlings will use dock A. I repeat dock A. Caniculiens will use dock B. Do not bring any of your belongings or medical supplies with you. The ships and their crews will provide everything you need."

The Tellurian children would be split between Earth and Canicula. Tellurians were the offspring of the mixed couples. They were named Tellurians in honor of the Earthlings who founded this project. Tellurian is anything that pertains to or inhabits the Earth. The mixed couples didn't approve of the idea of losing their children. They felt their children should go to the planet the parents chose. The couples had a major decision to make. It would affect them for the remainder of their lives.

Which planet should they call home? They could split and go to their own planets but they knew they'd never be happy separated. This was one decision Earthstar was leaving up to the couples. Neither world was sure how its inhabitants would feel about the Tellurians and their families.
Earthstar's citizens were anxious to return home. They didn't realize how much destruction was taking place on their planets.

Earthstar's rays would not affect Canicula. However, they had the same computers with nuclear devices that the Earth had. When Earthstar explodes the nuclear devices on Canicula would also explode. No one knew what kind of world the former inhabitants would be returning to. Only the healthy would be allowed to return home. The sick and the dead would remain on Earthstar. The citizens were issued protective suits. Earthstar's synthetic air was no longer safe to breathe. Professor Norvin's face appeared on the monitors once again.

"It's time my friends. Please make sure you are wearing your protective suits and helmets. Do not carry any belongings with you. Most of all don't panic! Sectors two-thirteen through two-fifteen please board the trams for the docking areas."

"Do not breathe the air. Do not panic. Do not leave your safety zones if your sectors have not been called. We will call your sector soon. There are only two ships docked now. They can't carry us all. The other ships will dock two at a time. Remember, dock A for Earthlings and dock B for Caniculiens."

The people opened their doors and glanced at the dark orange skies. The poisonous air was so thick with radiation they could actually see it moving. Earthstar no longer looked like Utopia. It looked like a war zone. The citizens from the designated sectors boarded the mini trams in an orderly fashion. Suddenly, people began running from all directions. The citizens had become mobs.

People from all sectors were trying to get to the docks. No one wanted to wait for his or her sectors to be called. They were rocking the trams trying to gain access. Some of the trams were turned over. Many people were injured or killed. It was Earth, all over again. The citizens were running like frightened rats. They pushed and shoved each other then walked on their fallen comrades. Children, husbands and wives were separated.

Earthstar shifted and most of the people fell creating small mounds of people. Those on the bottom were crushed. The two ships from Earth and Canicula moved into place to stabilize Earthstar. The Caniculien ship eased into dock B. The other ships positioned themselves in an opened arrowhead shape. They were assuming a docking position. When the other ships launched they would ease into position. To view the ships in formation was really quite amazing. The blue white lights on the outside of the ships lit up space brilliantly.

Toby and The Brain watched the ships from the helm of the Nebula II. The lights on the panel began to blink.

"Hey that's Morse code." Toby picked up a pencil. He slowly wrote the message down. The citizens have panicked. They will be storming the docks in less than twenty minutes. Brace yourselves. They are burning, looting and killing one another.

"Burning," Toby screamed. "I've got to get Mom's photo album. It's the only thing I have left to remember my family by."

"It will have to remain here." The Brain tried to comfort Toby.

"NO!" Toby yelled. "You don't understand. The deeds, keys and locations of everything are in that album."

I promised my Dad. I told him I would take care of it. The instructions on what I should do and whom I should contact, it's all there. I've got to get it. I'll be back before the ship leaves. Just hold my seat."

"No!" The Brain yelled. But before he could finish, Toby was gone.

Toby ran towards his old neighborhood. The streets were very crowded. It was difficult to tell which direction he was headed. He watched a strange man push a child into the streets. The man was running towards the docks, when a large metal beam crushed him. The child escaped injury.

"One of the lucky ones." A nurse said. She lifted the child into her arms. A smiling woman with a tear streaked face reached for the child. The nurse stepped over the beam and handed the child to the woman. The woman did not thank the nurse. She took the child and fled. A tall Caniculien stabbed another woman to get on the tram ahead of her.

Toby watched the senseless event without feelings. His feelings died with his mother. He reached his house within twenty minutes. Most of the neighborhood was burning or had collapsed. The doors had been ripped from his house. His mother's body was no longer in the window. He thought it was strange that his mother's body had been taken away but her clothing remained, bloody and lying against the window.

He ran downstairs into the safety zone. His mother had packed the family album in a white box with red polka dots on it. He searched through the rubble. It angered him that someone had ransacked his home. Why would someone desecrate his mother's final resting place? Why had someone taken her body? Why had they removed her clothing?

He had heard about people who used bodies for weird sexual perversive rituals. Maybe the Caniculiens took her body and removed the clothing. They could not put her in the pods with clothes on. The pods were capsules that froze the body. The capsules were then shot into space through a metal vacuum tube. Toby's mind was full of questions. He wondered if his father was on the Nebula II or if he was dead?

Toby found the white plastic box. The red dots reminded him of his mother's blood. He began to weep for his parents. He was not crying alone. The pleas and sobs of thousands of helpless souls echoed throughout the labyrinth of metallic sectors. But, the cries of the sick and helpless fell on deaf ears.

The sick were heavily sedated; so that no one would know they were alive. There were other cries that went unheard. Some couldn't be helped. Some wouldn't be helped. These were the cries of citizens trapped in their homes and other areas.

Technicians who had been working in the inner chambers were crushed to death by collapsing walls and falling beams. Small explosions in the life support sectors constantly threatened life on Earthstar. The technicians who managed to climb out of the tunnels and inner chambers did not try to help the ones who remained behind. The cries of the men who were still alive touched only one man. This man was ordered to ignore the cries or he too would be left behind.

People trapped in their buildings died trying to escape. Makeshift ropes with grappling hooks were thrown to the tops of buildings. People fell to their deaths when the ropes broke or the hooks slid out of place. Jumping into sheets held by others was just as fatal. People instituted mass suicides. Hypodermic needles filled with lethal doses of insulin and other medicines were passed around the buildings. Razor blades, knives, electricity and any other methods of suicide they could fathom were tried. They felt suicide was better than being blown to bits. Lifeless figures hung from windows, light fixtures and beams.

Many of the trapped citizens were determined to live. They tried to tunnel through walls to escape their hollow tombs. Strained voices, sore muscles and broken bones were the rewards for their futile efforts. Some citizens gathered in crowds and used their bodies to ram blocked doors. Some escaped, others were crushed to death.

Admiral Bradford stared at his instruments. His crew tried to rush the people on board the Nebula II without panicking them. They had to shoot mobs attacking the people trying to board the ship. He could not bear to watch the horrors. He was thankful his family was on board.

"Dad!" The Brain sounded worried. "Toby left the ship over an hour ago."

"Why did you let him leave?" Admiral Bradford asked. "He'd forgotten something his family told him not to lose. Please, Dad I'm fast and sneaky. I could get Toby and be back long before the Nebula II leaves the dock." The Brain pleaded.

"No! I've got you back and I'm not going to lose you again." The Brain knew his father was trying to protect him. "Please Dad, you know what an Explorer is capable of."

"Please dear, let him go." Mrs. Bradford knew her son would not be satisfied unless they let him try to rescue Toby.

"All right, but if you can't find him in twenty minutes then you come back alone." Admiral Bradford stated. "I promise. Thanks Dad. I love you and Mom too. If anything happens to me, remember I was happy because I died doing the same thing you are doing. I was trying to help someone else. Be proud Mom and Dad. You've taught me well. I'm an Explorer, Dad."

The Brain jumped onto the dock and ran towards Toby's house. He noticed several sectors burning out of control. Earthstar trembled constantly. The two ships were doing their best to stabilize her. But, The Brain knew Earthstar would not survive much longer. The gravity was nearly zero. The gravity was not a problem for people wearing protective suits. The boots they wore were weighted. Bodies that were once lying in the streets were now floating in the air.

Earthstar's interior structures were constantly collapsing and the pressure was becoming unbearable. The hottest areas were the top of the sphere and the side facing the sun. The air had become condensed and was not circulating. This caused the heat to intensify. The rising temperature and inevitable dehydration made breathing pure hell. Regulating the temperature was no longer possible. The temperature constantly shifted from the fires of hell to the great ice age.

The Brain watched as doctors and others left trapped people behind to die. They knew amputating an arm or leg would have freed some of the people. The trapped people yelled for someone to kill them and end their misery. The Brain ran down the streets of his

old neighborhood. He glanced around looking for
Toby. His mind was so occupied he nearly collided
with a crystalline stalagmite.

"What the hell is this?"

The small crystal rocks once scattered on the ground
had somehow fused together. The heat from the
friction created by Earthstar's rapid orbital decay
transformed the crystals into molten glass. When the
dripping glass cooled it was fused into stalagmites.
He glanced at the top of the sphere. He saw huge
stalactites hanging down.   A loud rumble came from
beneath his feet.

The pressure beneath the sidewalks pushed up until
the sidewalk was a small hill. The sidewalk began to
crack and crumble. The Brain jumped to the artificial
turf. The sidewalk continued crumbling block by
block. What was designed to be an extravagant place
for its future societies was quickly becoming a disaster
area. The areas designated for use by authorized
personnel only were no longer off limits. Explosions
had ripped the doors from their frames. They flew
through the air with such force they damaged
equipment and ruptured the walls of buildings.

Thinner doors and walls snapped like peanut brittle.
Laboratory animals ran wildly into the streets. Their
cages had been torn from the walls and strewn all over
the labs. Test tubes, beakers and flasks were piled in
broken heaps on the floor. Blackboards once covered
with equations were now charred and wrinkled from
the fires that seemed to be present in every sector of
Earthstar.

"My new manmade home is becoming a manmade time bomb." The Brain thought as he ran up the driveway to Toby's house. "Toby, where are you?" A loud crash echoed from the safety zone. Toby met him on the stairs.

"Brain, I found it." He held up the plastic box. "Somebody stole her. They took my Mom and left her clothing on the window sill." "I'm sure the medical team was here. They couldn't put her in the cryogenics tube with her clothes on."

"We've got to go Toby. The ships will be leaving soon. I'm not so sure the other ships will have time to load and take off before Earthstar blows."

The boys saw shredded portions of the wall hanging towards the ground in metallic strips. The bulbs and liquid diodes exploded without warning throughout the house.

"Let's get out of here, Toby." The Brain grabbed Toby and ran from the house. They watched clouds of steam puff through the sector walls scalding everyone who came in contact with it. An explosion caused a rift in an inner chamber. This prevented depressurization. Breathing became more of a hardship than a blessing. The planetoid shook for one brief moment then spiraled downwards like a spinning top. Everything not fastened down was thrown about with terrific force.

Chemicals in large quantities tipped over and mixed together. They formed toxic gases and acidic compounds. These compounds drifted out of the labs and into the atmosphere. Acid rains destroyed buildings, statues and everything else it touched. People screamed as the chemicals landed on their bodies. Soggy skin dripped from their skeletal faces. Toby and The Brain panicked. They ran towards the docks as fast as they could. It was impossible to see where they were going. The crowds quickly separated them.

"Toby," The Brain yelled.

His cries were futile. Toby was lost in the crowd. Toby made it to the front of the line. He hurried on board the ship. The doors closed behind him squashing a man's head. Toby sat in an empty seat next to a Caniculien girl named Chini. She was in his science class. He'd had a crush on her since the first day he'd seen her. She was dressed in a lavender dress trimmed in white and peach lace. Her hair was so white it was transparent. The lavender ribbons in her hair made her look angelic.

"I thought I'd never see you again. But here I am sitting next to you on the Nebula II. Wait a minute!" He yelled loudly. "This isn't the Nebula II. I am on the wrong ship. Oh God!"

Chini's parents turned around and looked at him. "Don't worry. We'll take good care of you." "Now we are your family," Chini smiled. "The two of us will always be together." Toby relaxed.
He liked the idea of a new family. He stopped hugging the plastic box and smiled.

The Brain reached dock A. "Hold the doors," he yelled. He made it through the doors before they closed.

"Your son is onboard." A crewman told the navigator. "Let's go sir." The Brain leaned against the door. He was too tired to move. One of the passengers fell against a red button. The doors slid open and The Brain fell out. A light flashed on the panel in front of Admiral Bradford. He pushed the button to seal the doors of the Nebula II. The Nebula II and the Caniculien ship left the docks. The other ships moved into docking position. The Brain knew he would never leave Earthstar. He walked back to his old neighborhood.

The light emitted from Earthstar was so intense it affected the accuracy of the ship's instruments. The ships used to stabilize Earthstar were reaching their limit on fuel. They would have to head home as soon as the next ships were loaded. The second set of ships to dock wondered whether to wait on the sectors called or to take the first people to get on their ships. Earthstar made that decision for them.

The green beacon blinked off in the environmental and life support systems. A red revolving light flashed on the outer hull of Earthstar. The planetoid's energy field changed and the orbit declined with the ships still docked. The planetoid was a sick patient with a migraine and a cancerous ulcer to match. The cancerous ailment had progressed to the terminal stage. It spread sector by sector until the disease could not be distinguished from the planetoid itself.

The increase in temperature from the internal unrest and the gravity of Earth pulling on it caused Earthstar to look like a golden sun. The more energy it absorbed the more it sent into outer space. It consumed and hungered for more even though it absorbed more than it could hold. The greed of the planetoid would be partially responsible for its demise. It had failed to completely dissipate heat and harmful radiation. This build up was melting the interior.

Contaminated water and food were no longer a problem for those who wanted to use them. They would only die a little quicker. The pumps on the oxygen converters were pumping too much oxygen through the air ducts. This helped the people to breathe better until Earthstar brushed against an asteroid. Earthstar began to rotate faster. No adjustments could be made to correct the situation. The constant jolting and spinning built up an enormous amount of friction. The friction produced heat and fused the tubes connected to pumps on the oxygen converters. The pressure began to build. The tubes burst and the converter began releasing pure oxygen into the atmosphere.

A live wire inside of the useless junk that was once Earthstar's onboard computers, generated a spark. The air in the room ignited. The flames burned the computer and a giant ball of fire engulfed the area. The Brain walked sadly down the crumbled sidewalk. He did not regret dying.

"Before I die, I'd like to know if anyone on Earth will survive. I'd also like to know if Toby is going to be okay."

Suddenly the sound of popping balloons surrounded him. Some of the protective suits were building up too much pressure. The suits got to a certain stage

and burst. Earthstar's gravity was about to hit zero.
The pressures were too much for the people especially
those not wearing protective suits. Their blood
pressures increased and their brains filled with blood.
The Brain watched a woman's eyes bulge out of their
sockets. He hoped they would not explode. The
woman's feet and legs began to swell. The water and
blood in her body was under a tremendous amount of
pressure. The Brain knew it wouldn't be long before
she exploded. People were breathing erratically.
Their lungs couldn't hold the oxygen. They would
either collapse or explode. A screaming man ran past
The Brain. His face had caved in. He stopped three
feet from The Brain, took a deep breath and then his
heart exploded. "I'm free," he whispered and then
died.

People bled from every orifice in their bodies. A
young boy standing in the middle of the street stared
blankly ahead. The Brain ran towards him. Before
he could reach him, the boys head popped. His body
stood headless for a few minutes and then dropped to
the ground. The boy had suffered a massive brain
hemorrhage.

"One thing Earthstar isn't lacking is blood. This
world is covered with it." The Brain ran up the
driveway to his house. He glanced behind him.
Blood and pieces of flesh were floating above the
heads of the citizens. Occasionally the gravity would
return and the people were drenched with blood and
flesh. The Brain knew there was only one thing for
him to do. The problem was how to do it. He
removed the debris from his front door. There was no
need to use his key card because the door had

splintered. He kicked the door and it crumbled. The
house was morbidly silent.
He was happy that his parents would not have to share
his fate.

"I'm no longer The Brain," he said. "I will die
Charles Bradford."

He walked into the dark kitchen. The refrigerator
door creaked loudly. He reached for the brown case
in back of the vegetable bin. This was his mother's
best-kept secret. The brown case contained small
bottles of Humulin R and N insulin and two syringes.
Charles entered his old bedroom. There he kneeled
on the floor and began to pray.

"Lord, what I am about to do is wrong. Please grant
my dying request. Forgive me for committing
suicide, allow me to see what happens to my family
and friends and allow me to die quickly."

He immediately fell into a deep sleep. He saw the
barren Earth. People were planting crops and
rebuilding cities. His family and friends declared him
a hero. He would be remembered forever as the
young man who saved the world. The scene changed.
He was looking at Canicula. Toby was with Chini
and her family. He was very happy and eventually
married Chini. They had two children. They named
the boy Charles.

Admiral and Mrs. Bradford started a transportation
service for their new world. They called it: Brain's
Flights and Motorized Transportation Services.
Charles awoke with a smile. God had answered his
prayers. The world would repopulate and the

Tellurian children would be accepted on both worlds. Both worlds would learn from their mistakes. Their future focuses would be on peace and acceptance.

He injected two hundred units of insulin into his arm. He crawled into a fetal position on his bed and waited for death to come. He died peacefully and instantly from a painless massive heart attack.

Earthstar's life support systems were failing. The pressure from the oxygen converter propelled a pipe through the air. The thrust was so great the pipe pierced the layers of Earthstar's walls and drifted into the emptiness of space. A red beacon blinked on a hidden transmitter on the outer hull. The transmitter sent a final signal to the nuclear computers on Canicula and Earth.

It instructed the computers to detonate their nuclear charges. A fiery ball escaped the life support systems. It ignited the atmosphere and everything it came in contact with. The citizens realized their lives were about to end.

The navigators heard an explosion in a distant airlock. They decided to disengage and head home. The crews were told to board the ships. The automatic doors closed killing many people. Some were cut in half by the doors. Half of their bodies were inside the ship the other halves dropped onto the docks. The instruments on the ships indicated a large amount of pressure building up in the environmental and life supports sectors. Oxygen and other miscellaneous gases were manufactured in these areas.

The pumps fused together while the machinery continued production. The pressure gauges read critical. Sparks created another ball of fire and the inner chambers exploded. The light from the planetoid's deadly halo was extinguished for a very brief moment. The green beacon no longer flashed. The remaining navigators and their crewmen knew something was terribly wrong.

They didn't have time to wonder what was wrong nor did they have time to lift off. The planetoid's red self-destruct beacon flashed on. Earthstar glowed with the radiance of the sun. Its rays reached into space like tentacles and grabbed the remaining ships. The ships and Earthstar exploded simultaneously.

The sound of the explosion could not be heard in the vacuums of space but the fire could be seen light years away. The golden ball of death was now flying through space in a million radioactive fragments. The people of Earth saw the dangerous metallic pieces as a large meteor shower.

Fragments plummeted the Earth, moon, Canicula and other heavenly bodies thousands of miles away. This was only the beginning of the world's troubles. The detonators had been activated and the nuclear holocaust was about to begin. Admiral Bradford established contact with Polaris' safety zones. He informed Dr. Cruz about Earthstar's demise.

"All of the ships including the stabilizers are gone. The Nebula II and the Caniculien ship carry the only survivors. Please give me further instructions."

Dr. Cruz responded. "All hell has broken loose here on Earth. Your best bet would be to bypass Earth and maintain orbit outside of the galaxy until Earthstar's fragments have passed you or disintegrated. I don't know how much damage will be done. The nuclear reactors and computers will be exploding at any time now. When you land wear protective suits. Try and reestablish contact in twenty four to forty eight hours." Admiral Bradford told his crew to explain the delay to the passengers. He also asked to see his son and wife.

The Nebula II passed by the Earth and continued outside the galaxy. Mrs. Bradford put her hands on her husband's shoulders.

She had tears in her eyes. "Where's Charles?" Her husband asked.

"He didn't make it." She said.

"But, he was onboard!" The Admiral yelled.

"I know. Someone accidentally hit the door's control panel and he fell off the ship."

"I closed my own son out!" Admiral Bradford became hysterical.

"You didn't know. Remember Rob. Remember what he told us. It's as if he knew all along. He gave his life for all of us and we're going to make sure everyone knows it."

They embraced and remembered their son's final words. The Bradford's tried to be strong. Tears filled their eyes. Charles was brave. He accepted his fate like a man. The Explorers would be very proud of him but not as proud as his parents.

Chapter 14-THE FINAL HOLOCAUST
A NEW BEGINNING!

The Caniculien ship landed safely. Medical teams met the survivors. Everyone was examined. They were then taken to the underground city. Toby glanced around the strange planet. Everything seemed to be red, gold and blue. The cold sand beneath his feet was light red. Above his head, the golden sky was filled with blue clouds. The strange buildings looked like red sand castles. They were odd but beautiful. The closer he got to the buildings, the more unusual they became. The red sand castles sparkled like opaque crystals.

They rode in strange rounded vans with tires similar to balloons. Chini said they would transfer to another vehicle soon because the rovers were not allowed on the streets. The streets were golden crystals with red dividing lines. The next vehicle was a small airship, which hovered above the street. It glided above the streets on a cushion of air.

Toby watched the scenery of his new world pass by. The trees had feathery leaves and the small bushes were furry. The streets were deserted. He knew the people were in the underground cities. Chini said her people had once lived thousands of miles beneath the ground. They voted to return to the surface the year her grandfather was born.

The airships stopped near slanted doors in the ground. The doors looked similar to the doors of a storm shelter. Chini pointed to an area beyond the doors.

"That is my home."

Toby looked at the sparkling blue sea beyond the houses. He had never seen water so blue and so clear. The planet seemed quite tranquil. He wished the Earth could be so peaceful. Two Caniculiens pushed the buttons on their small transmitters. The doors rolled back like a giant scroll. A wide set of escalators moved down into the subterranean city. Toby took a deep breath and shuddered. Chini's mother put her arms around him and smiled.

"You are now our son. Don't be afraid. We will protect you. We will do our best to make your parents proud. We know we can't replace your parents and we won't try to. We will simply be your adoptive parents. I will die for you as quickly as I would die for Chini."

She held his hand and they stepped onto the escalators together. They stepped off the escalators onto a golden sidewalk. The sidewalks moved automatically throughout the city.

"Where is the light coming from?" Toby asked.

 Glowing crystals lined the walls and ceilings beneath the planet. Lakes and waterfalls are beyond the city.

"Everything on the surface is also down here. Canicula is similar to Earth. But, it is also very different. "We have zoos. However, some of our animals are quite different from yours. Earth's, I mean. We don't have very many fast food restaurants."

"What will happen when the nuclear computers explode?" Toby asked.

"The surface will probably be destroyed. Canicula doesn't have nuclear reactors or plants. The damage want be as bad as it will be on Earth."

The Caniculien Society was the same as the United Nations. They decided it would be best to live underground for a few years. They wanted to make sure everyone learned from their mistakes. Everyone did not cooperate with the Caniculien Society. A few rebels decided to remain on the surface.

Chini said, "My Dad said they will not survive. Toby, do you think you can truly be happy on Canicula?"

Toby scratched his head. "It will take some getting used too. I will miss my friends. My family died on Earthstar. The Explorers were the only reason I wanted to return to Earth. My dream was to be a member of The Explorers Club. The Brain initiated me on Earthstar. It's ashamed I didn't get to join on Earth."

"You can meet new friends. We could start an Explorers Club." Chini smiled.

"No Chini. There's only one Explorers Club." Toby exclaimed.

"Wouldn't your friends be proud to know The Explorers Club had become interplanetary?" Chini exclaimed.

"Yeah!" Toby grinned. "I believe they would. How much danger are we in down here?"

"We are so far underground that we aren't in any real danger. After dinner, when our parents go to the town meeting; we can explore the city." Chini grinned.

"You said our parents!" Toby was shocked.

"Well they are. Aren't they?" Chini waited for an answer.

"Yeah!" Toby answered happily.

The underground world of Canicula was peaceful but the surface world was in turmoil. The nuclear computers exploded and a whirlwind of flames ravaged the surface. The Caniculiens who chose to remain on the surface began to panic. They were screaming and running blindly. Metallic fragments from Earthstar rained down on the Caniculiens. The radiation burned the vegetation. It caused lesions and cancerous sores to appear on the skin of the people and animals. Those who were lucky died from the flames of the nuclear explosion. Fish and other marine life floated on the surface of the waters.

The red sand castles were leveled by fiery winds. The waters were contaminated instantly. People huddled together in blazing masses. They looked like living campfires. Those leaning against rocks began to fuse with the rocks. The explosions sent out blinding lights. The optical lenses of the Caniculiens burnt to a cinder.

Mushroom clouds rose from the planet's surface. The sky turned a fiery orange. The radiation and contaminates were too much for the Caniculien's lungs. Their lungs began to burst. Blood flowed freely. People ran but there was no place to hide. The doors to the subterranean city had been sealed. They knocked on the doors in vain. The sound did not carry to the city below.

Husbands and wives caressed in fear. Their bodies fused together in a permanent hug. Everything the nuclear blasts didn't destroy, Earthstar's fragments did. The surface was now still. Those who chose to remain behind, no longer existed. Those who went below would be the future of the new world; a world that would exist below the surface for at least a decade.

Pam awoke in a damp drainpipe.

"How did I get here and where is Adam?"

She tasted blood. The pain in her head throbbed fiercely. There were cuts and bruises all over her body. Breathing was painful.

"I must have broken a few ribs. I've got to get out of this pipe." Her mind immediately flooded with memories.

She and Adam were in the helicopter with Wayne. A blinding beam swept across the sky towards them. They'd put on their parachutes in case they had to jump. A small plane flew between them and the beam. The plane exploded and the beam moved on. It hit a larger plane. The other plane exploded on contact. Their helicopter glowed white and became very hot from the ray. Adam kicked against the doors until they flew open, then Wayne put the helicopter on autopilot. Pam remembered looking down at a convoy of trucks below them. She glanced away for a brief moment. The next time she looked for them they were no longer there. Some of them had disintegrated, others had moved on. Adam kissed her then said I love you.

A few seconds later, he pushed her out of the helicopter. She thought she remembered Wayne and Adam jumping out behind her. But she wasn't quite sure. The air was stagnant and hot. Suffocating seemed inevitable. Before she could pull the ripcord on her parachute, the helicopter exploded. She remembered falling towards the Earth like a rocket. The ripcord instantly released the parachute.

"Pam! Pam!" Adam tried to scream her name above the noise of the explosion. She glanced up. Her parachute was on fire. That was the last thing she remembered.
 She had to get out of the pipe and find Adam. He would be worried about her. The pipe led in two directions, up and down. She chose up. The pipe ended below a large silver disc. She hammered her fist against the disc and yelled for help. Although the disc was made of a thin lightweight material, she could not lift it. "I know this material," she said.

"It's Synacom 14. But why can't I lift it?" She finally realized the disc must have been covered with debris. There was no alternative but to go in the opposite direction. The drainpipe ended twenty feet down. A tunnel large enough for her to walk in began at the end of the pipe. Stones lined the inside of the tunnel. She realized the tunnel was not manmade. It was natural. The tunnel was dark and she stumbled several times. The tunnel sloped downwards for miles and then leveled off.

Pam thought the tunnel would never end. She was beginning to get claustrophobic.

"I think I see a yellow speck of light ahead of me!" The tunnel turned sharply towards the left then continued downwards. "It must have been my imagination."

She had never been afraid of the dark. But after walking and stumbling in the dark for hours her fears were overwhelming. Once again she saw the yellow speck of light.

"Aw right, I may be hallucinating but I'm not crazy." The deeper she went the brighter the light became. "It's real! It must be a way out!"

The only problem with the light was she could now see the rats scampering across the rocks. "Oh God!" She took a painful deep breath then increased her pace. The tunnel began to widen. A lizard scurried across her shoe. The interior of the tunnel was becoming cold and wet. A jagged stone ripped through the soft flesh of her hand. Blood oozed from the wound.

Pam slipped on the wet surface and gashed her head. The once clotted blood began to run freely. The tunnel began to spin and pain encompassed her body. She forced herself to move closer and closer towards the light. The water in the tunnel was now waist deep. Ahead she heard the sound of running water. Using the sides of the tunnel as a crutch, she worked her way towards the end of the tunnel.

"It's a small waterfall!" She exclaimed.

The bright light had led her into a large cavern. The waterfall emptied into a crystal lake. The bottom of the lake was covered with small glittery objects. The water was deep enough to dive into. She did more of a weak fall than a dive. Her body pierced the surface of the tranquil lake. The cool water cleared her head. Pam swam wearily towards the shore. Exhausted, she dragged herself onto a smooth rock. Cupping her hands she began to drink the cool water. "I didn't realize how thirsty I was."

A campfire glowed less than twenty feet away. "Now how did that get down here? Adam. Adam must be here somewhere." She stumbled towards the campfire and warmed her hands. The fire had warmed the stone floor near it. She laid down to rest. Her head ached and her fingers were numb. She wiped the blood from her forehead and drifted to sleep.

"I told you there were fish here." Reggie carried a line with twenty fish tied to it.

He couldn't wait to scale, clean and cook them. The Explorers were quite comfortable in their new surroundings. Thoughtful packing and good minds came in handy. The girls were ready to help prepare the meal. They were hungry and prepared for anything, well not quite anything. Nothing could have prepared them for what they found a few feet away.

"There's something by the fire!" Tia pointed to a curled figure lying close to the fire. "It looks like a person, but how? No one passed us. The entrance is behind us."

"Maybe," Steffie added. "Maybe the person is dead and washed up on the shore."

"That's impossible. The current isn't that strong. Besides, the fire is at least twenty feet from the water." Reggie said, shaking his head.

The Explorers saw the person move. They ran towards the fire.

"It's Pam!" Nick gasped. "And she's alive!"

Max ran to get the first aid kit. Nick shook Pam. She thought she was still dreaming or hallucinating.

"N-Nick is it really you?"

"Yes, it's me Pam. In fact most of The Explorers are here. Max is bringing the first aid kit. We'll bandage your head and hands. We've caught some fish. So after a hot meal and some medicine, you can tell us how you got here."

Tia and Angie Faye cleaned and dressed Pam's wounds. Angie Faye opened cans of baked beans while the boys prepared the fish.

The food tasted as good as it smelled. None of them realized how famished they really were until they tasted the food. Pam glanced in the Explorers' first aid kit. She knew they had come prepared. After dinner she told them her story and asked why they were not in Polaris' safety zone. The Explorers quickly explained their hypothesis to her.

The temperature near the water was dropping. A strange wind was blowing from somewhere. Pam followed the Explorers to their sleeping area, which was three levels above the water. The temperature was more tolerable at that level. They passed out sleeping bags, blankets and inflatable pillows.

"Do you have an extra blanket?" Pam asked.

Mike smiled. "Does a bear shit in the woods?"

The Explorers always carried extra supplies. He handed Pam a sleeping bag, pillow and blanket. A fire blazed a few feet away from their sleeping area. They appeared to be happy but they were all worried about their families and friends. They wondered if anyone above the surface would still be alive when the disaster ended. They knew the computers would explode soon.

Fragments from Earthstar's explosion flew in all directions. The mobs and the others who chose to avoid the safety zones and caves saw a spectacular light show. The falling debris looked like gigantic fireworks that would not disintegrate. The people watched a large white and gold flower bloom. The closer it came to Earth; the wider the petals opened. Crystal seeds were expelled from the center of the flower. The elongated diamond shaped crystals headed directly towards them. Hot molten metal began to rain upon the Earth. The sky darkened. Everything was silent. The wind refused to blow and the rain stopped falling. An old man glanced up at the sky. "This is the calm before the storm." He was right. A storm more horrendous than anyone could imagine was brewing over the horizon.

A violent explosion shook the Earth. One by one the nuclear computers began to explode. The cities and surrounding areas were leveled. A giant radioactive cloud appeared above the Earth's horizon. The wind began blowing wildly. Nuclear reactors exploded around the world. One by one disaster struck the nuclear plants like the domino effect. Rains of hot molten metal mixed with the nuclear fallout.

Earthstar's debris pounded the Earth like basketball sized hail. Everything touched by the gigantic pieces of hot alien metal was destroyed. Man, animal, vegetation and buildings began to disintegrate. It was as if they never existed. People died in many horrible ways. Perhaps there was still some degree of justice left in the world. The mobs that killed others would now die themselves.

The sun was still shining above the Earth but it could not be seen. The Earth's skies were covered with blankets of contaminated clouds. Radioactive fires raged around the world. Beautiful monuments that were once symbols of man's achievements were now dust blowing on the winds.
 The devastating blasts of global explosions put an end to the riots and strife. The lightning performed beautifully but no one wished to watch its performance. This lightning was not cause by the radiation from Earthstar. It was due to the high electrical energy, which was used to generate Earthstar's magnetic field.

 The clouds above the Earth absorbed the charges. When the wind's velocity increased the clouds collided. The heavily charged clouds created forked lightning. It hurled towards the Earth striking people and objects without prejudice. Heat and solar radiation interacted with the atmosphere to create an unusual phenomenon.

Dangerous balls of fire zipped through the air and across the Earth. The fireballs along with the lightning wreaked havoc around the world. Tidal waves, earthquakes and other natural disasters participated in destroying civilizations. Ancient pyramids that once stood the test of time, no longer existed. The smell of decomposing bodies and burnt flesh filled the air but there was no one left to smell it.

Remnants of fused flesh and skeletal frames were like petrified stone. The nuclear explosion weakened the Earth causing many structures to sink deep into the ground becoming buried forever. The majority of the Earth's surface was barren. The Earth looked like a large desert cluttered with debris. The only surface movement in these areas was the occasional strong gusts of wind produced by the nuclear holocaust. The scientist studied their monitors. Their instruments monitored the destruction above the ground and the shelters beneath it. It appeared as if everything that remained on the surface of the Earth had died. The computers proved them wrong. There were areas not exposed to the radiation. Those people, plants and animals were still alive.

"I guess the human; plant and animal species will have to be repopulated by those survivors and the ones in the shelters." Dr. Quartz smiled.

She knew the I.S.S.A didn't build enough shelters to provide housing for everyone. Two thirds of the Earth's population died needlessly. The I.S.S.A planned to save only the amount of people they believed they could control. They wanted to form a worldwide dictatorship but their plan was not to be. The shelters were thought to be indestructible because they were made of Synacom 14. The scientists and inhabitants of the shelters would soon learn what Nicholas Cruz II already knew.

The constant stress from external forces created by the natural disasters caused some shelters to sink. Several shelters were submerged under water due to earthquakes and tidal waves. The shelters were subjected to an unusual amount of pressure and exploded. Very few people survived. The survivors used debris from the shelters to reach the land.

Artificial bolts of lightning constantly hit shelters in the highly energized areas. The Synacom 14 absorbed too much energy and couldn't dissipate all of it. This constant exposure and over absorption caused the shelters to disintegrate. Some shelters were only partially affected. Their survivors were capable of escaping. These survivors searched for other areas to hide. A few shelters were plagued with intense heat and pressure outside the shelters. The heat evaporated the air inside and the inhabitants suffocated.

Synacom 14 is only soundproof from outside noises to a certain degree. The sound of rumbling aftershocks, volcanic eruptions and intense lightning strikes were audible. The people were extremely frightened. They were informed about the cracked and sinking shelters.

"All radioactive substances decay at various rates of speed. The heat will decrease when the energized particles have used up most of their charges. The clouds will then produce near normal rain. Our instruments will tell us when it is safe to return to the surface. It may take years to rebuild what has been destroyed but together we can accomplish anything."

"We are the future." Dr. Cruz mopped his brow with a handkerchief then continued. "The computers show new land masses adjacent to islands and peninsulas. This is due to the cooling lava. The windstorms are beginning to carry pumice and other minerals in the form of volcanic ash. This will be the basis for rich soil once the danger has passed." The people sat quietly while Dr. Cruz spoke.

They knew the world they loved no longer existed. The only way to survive in this new world would be to work together. They would have to set aside prejudice and bickering. Cooperation, trust and hard work would be essential. The same elements, which destroyed the vegetation and life around the world, now provided the necessary tools to give rebirth to the lifeless surface.

Months later Dr. Cruz stood before the people again.

"It has started raining naturally. The ocean waves and rains are washing portions of the radioactive topsoil out to sea. We have not been able to contact the other shelters. Therefore, we don't know how many survivors are left. We have kept in contact with the Nebula II. They suffered no damage from Earthstar. All old forms of government are now obsolete. It is going to be up to you to decide whether we rebuild together as one nation or whether we divide."

Dr. Cruz walked back to his office. He wondered if the world had needed a good cleansing and a new start. In the shelters people were struggling emotionally and stress mounted. They were afraid each malfunction or accidental death would lead to their destruction. The I.S.S.A were the temporary leaders of the people. The people were told without an organized government they would panic and act like the mobs. The people had no idea how much time had passed. Day and night were determined by the activities of the scientists and the data retrieved from the computers. They weren't sure if the data they were given was right or wrong.

The people living in the caves had good sources of uncontaminated water. There was no way for them to test the food they packed unless they had pets. The caves provided suitable shelter with room to move about freely. Some of the caves had mushrooms and other edible vegetation growing in them. Insects and other life forms shared the caves too.

The sound of the caves reminded the people of the surface. They heard water splashing and crickets chirping. The spider's cobwebs were larger and more intricate. Underground gases were known to seep into these places. Some were harmless. Others were poisonous or combustible.

Weakened places were subject to cave-ins. These areas generally had small mounds of debris on the cavern floor. The cave dwellers carbide lanterns would act as warning beacons. When dangerous fumes are present the flames from the lanterns, campfires and torches would change colors.

Canicula still functioned as a complete planet. They still enjoyed the comforts below the surface that were above it.   Their scientists had been trying to think of a way to help the Earthlings.   Dr. Telafist paced around the laboratory.

"There must be a way to render radioactive materials harmless without waiting.   The earthlings don't possess the knowledge to do this.   I know that nature has a way of cleansing itself of almost anything that upsets its delicate balance. But that takes so long. Maybe someday a study involving transuranic substances and matter anti-matter will provide the answers to this problem."

 Professor Felzman interrupted. "Perhaps rearranging the subatomic particles or the way the energy is released…"

"Yes it is possible.   The transuranic fuel can provide the answer."   Dr. Telafist interrupted.

"If we can invent a synthetic rod of transuranic crystal and build a laser that could change the harmful radiation into another form of energy…   We could determine the length of time for the ray to take affect by figuring half the radioactive life of different contaminates.   You see."   Dr. Telafist rubbed his chin.

"The first half of the process will have to be done in outer space.   We could also close the wormhole created by Earthstar.   The reflective disks and mirrors should be made of Synacom 14.   Our ships will carry these items to the desired locations.   Once the wormhole has been sealed, we can surround the Earth and bombard it with transmuting rays. The spherical shape of the disks will allow us to cleanse large amounts of surface areas in a matter of minutes."

The two scientists presented their theories to the council. They were granted permission to begin work immediately. Their plan would save Earth, Canicula and other worlds in the future. These scientists and their staffs worked many long hard hours. They made many mistakes. It only took two weeks to complete the project and launch the ships towards the wormhole and Earth.

It didn't take long for them to seal the wormhole. Less than an hour later the Caniculiens focused their rays and the Earth was engulfed in a visible illumination of transuranic energy. The clouds above the Earth exhibited an array of colors. Earth's waters refracted the light and reflected it into the air.

A beautiful rainbow appeared around the Earth. The transmutation of both matter and energy worked together to breathe life into a dying planet. The same principles of Physics that created this catastrophe were now repairing the damage. The depressed people of Earth were still praying for a better day when the first signs of a new Earth dawned over the horizon.

Scientists and technicians were glued to their computers. They watched with awe as the Caniculien's ships began to redeem the Earth. The people knew something was happening because the scientists and techs were ignoring them. They demanded to know what was happening. Dr. Cruz explained what the Caniculiens were doing. The people were ecstatic. They cheered and celebrated. The Earth's soils and waters would be back to normal but the hard part had yet to come. The people would have to cultivate the land and rebuild the cities.

Citizens around the world were looking forward to the task.

It would be difficult but well worth the effort. Only this time, they had no intention of letting one group hold all the authority and power. The world, the new world would be for all people, not just the brains and the elite.

The circular doors on the bottom of the Caniculien ship slid open. Bright blue beams with gold sparkles encircled the Earth. Animal carcasses and human remains transformed into balls of light then disappeared. Several Caniculien ships participated in the Earth's clean-up project. A square probe surveyed the lands and the waters. It tested them for contaminates.

Submersible ships dove into the oceans and seas. They traveled great distances to cleanse the waters of Earth. All traces of the dead and contamination were vanquished. They also repaired the damage done to the ocean floor. Fault lines were sealed. Debris and other dangers were removed. The alien teams worked feverishly to restore the Earth to its original state. Uncontaminated waters began to evaporate and form clouds.

Thunder roared, lightning flashed and torrents of clean fresh rain fell to the Earth. The Earth was reborn. The navigator of the alpha ship contacted Polaris' safety zone.

"The Earth is clean. It is now up to your people to cultivate the land with the unique vegetation that made this planet a wonder to behold."

The areas that avoided radiation were also cleansed.

"You have a new world with no pollutants, smog, wars or disease. It is up to you to keep it this way. We have captured healthy specimens of livestock, fish and fowls from your planet as well as ours to repopulate the Earth. We have also provided you with bags of plants and vegetables from both worlds."

"The direction your new technology takes should be determined by your new societies. I hope you can find peace among yourselves and rebuild a world built on love and lasting peace. It's time for us to correct the problems of our own society. We will remain underground even though our surface will be cleansed. We have a lot to learn. There is so much we did not know about the effects of nuclear power and the effects of too much power. The Tellurians and Earthlings on Canicula will be treated as Caniculiens. We will keep in contact with you for as long as you are a healthy and peaceful planet. Good luck and long life to you."

The ships blasted off into outer space. Both worlds had gone through a lot and the future was now ready to be molded. The Nebula II was instructed to land. The shelters opened their doors. A clear blue sky greeted them. The rain had passed and so had the danger. The inhabitants of the shelters stood on the moist fertile soil. The people thought something was wrong with the air. This was the first time they had inhaled unpolluted air.

The pure oceans were so clear they could see the ocean floors. Fish of known and unknown species swam peacefully together. Different species of animals walked side by side across the land. The people stared in awe. They were witnessing the beginning of a new world. They were the Adams and Eves. Only their Garden of Eden was bare.

Large sacks of seeds were stacked on the ground around the world. Tools rested against the sacks. A large photo album rested on top of the soil. The albums contained the names of the dead, their races and the planet they came from. Mourning the dead would have to come later. The people had a lot of hard work ahead of them.

They grabbed tools, wheelbarrows and sacks of seeds. Several people sat on the ground. They drew plans for planting gardens and other vegetation. No one would have believed the different people of the world could work so well together. Blacks, Whites, Chinese, Africans, Caniculiens and other races and creeds worked together as one.

The people living in caves sensed an unusual calm above the surface. They peered out of the caves. The world was barren but peaceful. These people walked quietly towards the sounds of laughter. One by one they joined the ranks of the new world. Pam and the Explorers had also sensed the calm.

Reggie climbed out of the cave. He stood on the top of the hill above the cave.

"The world is barren but the soil is so fertile. The world we once knew is gone. There are no buildings or structures of any kind. It's like the world and man has been given a second chance. I hope we use it

wisely because I'm afraid we will not get a third
chance."

They packed up their gear and climbed down the steep
hill. A pile of sacks stood beneath the hill. They
read the labels. Tools were lying on the ground a few
feet away. Pam picked up the photo album. She
glanced through it.

"Come on Pam," Nick yelled. "We've got to make it
to the place where Polaris Town once stood."

Pam closed the album and tucked it under her arm.
They walked in the direction they assumed would lead
them to the non-existent town called Polaris. They
weren't sure how much time had
passed. The radiation had stopped their watches
before they entered the caves. The moist soil stuck
to their tennis shoes.

"Wow, this is real air. I mean it's pure. There's no
trace of pollution. What do you think happened?"
Max asked.

None of them knew exactly what had happened.
Their world should have been in shambles. Pollution
and debris should have been scattered everywhere.
Where were the bodies? Why was the soil and air so
perfect? Reggie had seen people cultivating the land.
They wondered if the fresh air and the high altitude
had temporarily affected his mind. Tia was tired. She
remembered the caves were twenty miles from Polaris
Town.

"Twenty miles! We have to walk twenty miles."
The terrain was clear but the thought of walking

twenty miles depressed Tia. They walked seven miles and sat down to rest. The sun was going down. Getting lost was the last thing they wanted to do. Max arranged their sleeping bags in a circle. They were actually going to sleep under the stars like in the old westerns. Steffie passed out crackers, potted meat, cupcakes, beef jerky and potato chips. They ate and tried to figure out what had happened while they were in the caves.

"Maybe," Angie Faye gasped. "We are the only people left on Earth. Well, us and the people Reggie saw. If there were others, we would have run into them by now." Her statement was worth thinking about.

"Perhaps the Caniculiens came here and cleaned up the radiation." Reggie raised his hands in the air. "They could have zapped all the radiation and debris then disintegrated the remaining particles."

"You know, Reggie," Nick grinned. "It could have really happened that way."

The sunset and the stars lit up the sky. It was extremely dark without streetlights. Pam and the Explorers were experiencing the things their great-great grandparents had talked about. The sky was so clear. The full moon glowed brightly. Everyone wondered if the world would remain this way or if the future technology would ruin the natural beauty.

They fell asleep to the sound of wolves baying at the moon. Mike was so uncomfortable. The sun was so bright and the temperature inside his sleeping bag had risen. He put his hands in front of his face to shield it from the bright sunshine. The position of the sun told him it was almost noon.

"It's time to get up guys. It's almost noon."

Pam and the Explorers slowly came to life. They could not believe they had slept so late.

"I guess the sounds of this serene world rocked us gently to sleep and our bodies took advantage of it." Nick stood and stretched.

Breakfast consisted of Twinkies and potato chips. They sipped their water carefully. They did not want to run out. Once there gear was packed, they started walking towards Polaris. The sounds of laughter were carried on the wind. Three miles from their destination, the sounds became more audible.

"We're almost there. I guess we can take a few minutes break."

They sat on the drying soil. Pam opened the photo album. She read the first four pages.

"I don't believe this!" She told the Explorers. "More than two thirds of the Earth's population died. Several I.S.S.A shelters were destroyed. You were right Reggie. The Caniculiens did cleanse the Earth and its atmosphere. They also repopulated the animals of the world. People around the globe will have to repopulate the world. God, this is so exciting. These photo albums were placed in communities everywhere. This one contains the dead from the Enich Hills area. They are listed in alphabetical order."

Pam recognized several friends and neighbors. Sadly she reported the death of Charles Bradford, the Brain. The explorers were devastated and yet they were proud of their friend. Pam scanned the H's. There was no Wayne Hillard. She felt relieved. She was about to finish the R's when Nick announced it was time to move on. She glanced quickly at the remainder of the R's and the S's. Her mouth fell open. She tried to speak but no words came from her lips

"What's wrong with Pam?" Angie Faye asked.

Nick Kneeled beside Pam. She was staring at something in the photo album. Nick removed Pam's hand from the album. He looked at the photographs on the two pages. The last picture on the page was Dr. Adam Stanton of Canicula.

"Adam was a Caniculien! Oh man. Wow, no one knew!" Nick realized that Pam hadn't known either.

"Oh Nick, you were right. We could have saved the world. Adam's dead. Oh God, Adam's dead." She cried aloud.

Nick realized Pam still hadn't paid attention to the fact that Adam was a Caniculien. Angie Faye gave Pam a sedative. Two hours later Nick told Pam about Adam. Pam stood up.

"Let's go. We've got to get to Polaris Town."

Pam walked ahead of the Explorers. She dropped her head as the life within her jumped for joy.

EPILOGUE

What began as a chance for humanity to receive great knowledge and scientific advancements had become a race against death. Earth's people had learned a new definition for the word "Destruction!" As early man feared the comet and shuddered at the thought of it; so shall the survivors of this disaster shudder when they remember Earthstar and the events that followed it. Generations on both planets must learn to overcome prejudice, hate and injustice.

The Pope was wrong. The Tellurian children were not monsters from a heathen place. They were simply children. The survivors would soon realize through wisdom, open minds and loving hearts that these children could be part of the solution to one of humanities oldest problems…"Racism!"

For thousands of years mankind has allowed its prejudice to maim and destroy what man failed to understand or did not care to. The secret in his dark heart caused him to oppress anyone different from himself. What thousands of years of hate, distrust and oppression has done to destroy the world; generations of love must change to rebuild it.
 The prejudice of man's heart is a web that ensnares all who follow its bitter example. The thread of the web is our ignorance of others. Exposure to other cultures and the wisdom to keep an open mind will help to dispel the fears and misconceptions that divide all people.

When civilized man comes to this realization; it will make "The Golden Rule" an instrument to promote peace!

www.ingramcontent.com/pod-product-compliance
Lightning Source LLC
Chambersburg PA
CBHW072222170626
46813CB00003B/1060